Pride's Spell

Prince's Spell

ALSO BY MATT WALLACE

THE SIN DU JOUR SERIES
Envy of Angels
Lustlocked

THE SLINGERS SAGA
Slingers
One Fall to Finish
The Victim Hold
Where Gods Cannot See
Savage Weapons

The Failed Cities
The Next Fix

PRIDE'S
SPELL

MATT WALLACE

A TOM DOHERTY ASSOCIATES BOOK
NEW YORK

PRIDE'S SPELL

Copyright © 2016 by Matt Wallace

Cover photo by Getty Images
Cover design by Peter Lutjen

Edited by Lee Harris

A Tor.com Book
Published by Tom Doherty Associates, LLC
175 Fifth Avenue
New York, NY 10010

www.tor.com

Tor® is a registered trademark of Tom Doherty Associates, LLC.

ISBN 978-0-7653-9001-1 (ebook)
ISBN 978-0-7653-9000-4 (trade paperback)

First Edition: June 2016

PART I

SIN DU JOUR GOES HOLLYWOOD

PROLOGUE:
BRONKO IN HELL

The lights burn brighter than any layperson can imagine, but Bronko is used to sweating in kitchens far hotter than this studio. Besides, he belongs here just as much as he belongs over the open flame of a commercial stove, plying the trade and practicing the craft he loves more than he's ever loved anything.

The set behind him is a life-sized diorama of a rustic farm kitchen, complete with a window staring out over a painting of a Southwestern desert plain at dusk. He's wearing a chef's smock as jet-black as a shocktrooper's uniform, with silver dollar–sized buttons of polished brass. The logo of his Deadman's Hand gastropub chain, a meat cleaver piercing five playing cards fanned out to reveal the infamous aces-and-eights poker hand that was dealt to "Wild Bill" Hickok before he was shot and killed, is stitched onto the breast.

Bronko stares out past the television cameras and crew at a bandstand filled with a smiling studio audience. They're all shiny, attractive couples in their mid- to late twenties; they're so shiny, in fact, that their hair and skin all look like plastic. Their teeth are also so white and exposed it's almost like a sea of giant pupil-less eyes staring back at him. Each couple wears the same sweater in a kaleidoscope of sickeningly pastel colors.

There's a voice somewhere in the spare corners of his mind shouting at him that these people don't just look like plastic, they are plastic. What's more, if he were possessed of his everyday awareness Bronko might notice he's not looking at a hundred couples, he's looking at fifty exact replicas of one couple. Of course, if he were really aware he'd remember that the show he's about to tape a brand-new episode of was canceled more than fifteen years ago.

Yet somehow on the surface it all seems normal to him, the way the most absurd and surreal events seem perfectly normal in a dream. He ignores the voice and its distracting assertions, going over the recipe for the dish he's demonstrating in his head.

"You ready, Bronko?" a director in a baseball cap secured to his skull by a headset asks him from beyond the perimeter of cameras.

Bronko just nods, forcing that nagging sensation that something is wrong, all wrong with this into a locked box in the back of his mind.

He clears his throat and pastes a show-business smile across his lips.

The director counts down from five and cues him, and a red light lets him know which camera to play to and when.

"Folks, welcome back to the ol' Double-Cross Ranch!" Bronko greets the viewing audience through the camera's lens. "Now, if you're like me, you're a damn handsome man and the only thing you like more than hosting a big throw-down for all your friends on game day is the party snacks you put out for that throwdown. Am I right?"

The laughter of the studio audience is a mechanical chorus that's exaggerated far beyond anything natural or even human.

Again that inner voice insists this is all wrong, and again Bronko ignores it.

He's playing to his public, after all.

Bronko spreads his arms above the countertop in front of him with its custom burners, cutting board, and a diverse assortment of ingredients.

"Now, one of Bronko's ol' party favorites, and one that's always a crowd pleaser on Super Bowl Sunday, brings together two of my favorite things: Chinese take-out and down-home Western cooking."

Again, that clucking, forced laughter from the audience.

"We're going to be making pulled pork egg rolls with a sweet onion and pear barbeque sauce. They're gonna be bite-sized, perfect for grabbing and gulping, and you won't be able to keep 'em on a platter, trust me. Now, you'll notice I don't have my protein prepped and ready to go here. That's because we've got a big treat for y'all today. Ya see—"

Bronko pauses, quite uncustomarily for the polished performer he's become. There's a sudden dread welling up from deep in his guts, bubbling with an acid tinge that feels like it's souring his entire being.

That voice he's been shuttering and ignoring is screaming at him not to say the next words of the script he himself always wrote.

"Ya see," Bronko presses on, insisting to himself this is all as it should be, "today I'm going to show you how to butcher and process from your own whole pig. It's the ultimate party king move. Or queen move, ladies, we are partyin' in the new millennium, after all. Bring it on out, boys!"

Bronko looks offstage, the dread having risen to his chest, where it's formed a vice around his heart.

Two attendants whose entire heads are draped in cloth executioner's hoods wheel out a stainless-steel gurney.

The dread hits Bronko's brain like a high wave and breaks the prison he's constructed for that voice of warning.

It's not a pig that's being borne upon the cold metallic surface of that gurney.

It's him. It is Bronko's own dead body, stripped down and shaved bare, dressed as one would dress a whole pig for butchering. The perfect copy of his form is split right down the middle and has obviously been scraped of its internal organs.

The plastic crowd applauds enthusiastically.

His director gives him a grin and a thumbs-up.

The reality of the situation gnaws painfully on the back of Bronko's consciousness like the most inconvenient truth.

Bronko takes up his largest kitchen knife, a gleaming Kauffman with a Damascus blade the size of a small machete's. Walking on wobbly knees, he moves from around his cooking station to stand above the gurney. He holds the tip poised above the dry slit opened through his doppleganger's chest and stomach.

"Now, I . . . uh . . . what you wanna do here, folks, is you wanna . . ."

He can feel sweat pouring from his head now. His heart is pounding like an angry gorilla's fist against the inside of his chest. His pulse is so high he can almost feel every single drop of blood in his body raging through his veins. Bronko concentrates on the tip of the blade, trying not to see what's beyond it, what he's about to cut into.

"You just start . . . you just . . ."

That's when the corpse that is him draws a deep, sudden, painful breath.

Bronko drops his knife, the first time that's happened since he was an apprentice chef, and backs away from himself on the slab.

The crowd collectively gasps.

In the next moment he's running, like an animal, crashing through the back of the set and stumbling over equipment and hollow-eyed crewmembers.

He spots a red door in the darkness, the only one in sight. It must be the exit, and at worst it's an exit from this horrific place. Bronko bolts toward it, arms and legs pumping and breath coming in ragged pants.

Reaching for the handle, his body collides with the door and forces it open before he's even turned the knob. He bursts through to the other side and throws the door shut behind him. He stumbles a few more frantic strides before halting himself, doubling over and grasping his knees, overtaken by a hacking cough for several moments before he can lift his head and focus his eyes.

He's met by the enthusiastic applause of the same plastic pastel audience he just escaped.

Bronko is back on his old kitchen set. He glances over his shoulder. The door he just crashed through is gone. Looking back, he sees the director waving him frantically toward his prep and cooking station with its painted Southwestern desert background.

The panic that owned him just a moment before becomes an eerie calm that is slowly replaced by icy resolve.

The voice that broke loose and was only a moment ago screaming inside his skull is snuffed again into silence.

Bronko stands tall and sucks in a deep breath, the exhale

carrying him back to his mark.

"Welcome to the Double-Cross Ranch, folks," Bronko greets the crowd once more, as if he hadn't just fled the same inhuman audience. "We've got a real treat for y'all today, let me tell you . . ."

DOMESTIC SQUABBLES

Darren sits on the secondhand couch of the apartment he and Lena share on the edge of Williamsburg, eating Marshmallow Magic cereal from a chipped ceramic bowl.

He's spent most of the morning binge-watching a season's worth of DVRed episodes of the El Rey Network's *Lucha Underground*, a surprisingly successful reinvention of traditional Mexican pro-wrestling.

Since he and Lena began working at Sin du Jour less than two months ago, their bank accounts have already made what was once a long uphill trudge into the black, but their free time is almost nonexistent.

Also, he's been nearly eviscerated in a battle between rival demon clans, he helped maim a real-live angel, met God incarnate, and turned into a reptilian lust monster that tried to kill all his coworkers.

Darren doesn't remember much about that last part, but he remembers some . . . some . . .

As for the rest, he tries to focus on the wondrous, bloodless parts of the overall experience.

He grew up in the Midwest.

He's good at repressing shit.

He's on his third bowl of cereal and fourth episode of *Lucha Underground* when Tag Dorsky walks out of the hallway leading to Darren's and Lena's bedrooms.

Dorsky is wearing a T-shirt and jeans and looks freshly showered.

It's the first time Darren has seen Sin du Jour's sous-chef out of his kitchen whites. Hell, it's the first time he's seen him outside work.

It is not, however, the first time Darren has *heard* him outside of work.

Darren could hear both Dorsky and Lena last night through the wall separating their bedrooms.

Darren didn't sleep much.

"Well," Dorsky says, pausing beside the couch. "This is awkward."

"Yeah," Darren agrees.

Dorsky looks over at the TV screen, briefly watching legendary wrestler Vampiro as he gives an impassioned speech into a microphone.

"Do you speak Spanish?" he asks Darren, who shrugs.

"When I was three my dad took me to Mexico to stay with our relatives down there for the summer. When I came back I guess I wouldn't speak anything *but* Spanish. For like, a whole year. I lost most of it, though. My mom never wanted to learn."

Dorsky nods vacantly. Whether he was actually listening is anyone's guess.

He stares at the TV for another few seconds, and then: "Aw'right. Well. I'll see you on the line. Maybe let's not talk in the kitchen about how we all started our day. Cool?"

"Yeah. Sure."

"Cool."

Dorsky leaves their apartment.

After he's gone, Darren leans forward and sets his bowl on their living room table.

He's finally lost his appetite.

Fifteen minutes later, Lena staggers out into the living room, still half-asleep.

"Did you make coffee?" she asks.

"No."

She heads into their kitchenette. "Stupid question, I guess."

Darren listens to her rattling things around, pulling out her kettle, grinder, filter, and pour-over dripper as she prepares to turn the Kenyan beans they bought at the farmers' market into coffee.

He pretends to watch the show for another few minutes before asking, "So, are you two like, a thing now?"

"What do you mean?"

"You know what I mean."

In the kitchenette, Lena shrugs. "No. We're not a 'thing,' whatever that means."

She finishes the precision pour-over she insisted on learning to do better than any barista in their neighborhood, leaning over their small bar and sipping from her mug gratefully.

"Do you think it's a good idea? He's a sous-chef."

Lena frowns into her mug. "Is there anything normal about where we work, Darren? For chrissakes, last month you turned into a lizard and tried to fuck both him and me to death."

"I don't want to talk about that!" Darren snaps. "And whatever anyway, we still have to work there. What's the line going to think?"

"I'm way past caring what testosterone goobers on the line think of me. No matter what I do, who I screw or don't screw; it's always going to be the same. So, to hell with them. I thought you'd have learned that by now, at least. After everything that happened at Porto Fiero after . . ."

Lena trails off, sighing, realizing she's about to go too far and letting the past invocation die on her lips.

It's also obvious Darren wants to talk about the incident at the Michelin-starred Manhattan restaurant that got them fired and blackballed in the city less than he wants to talk about his time as a sex lizard.

"I just . . . I thought you hated him."

"My opinion of him is not much improved now," Lena mutters.

"Then what? I mean, if he didn't respect you before do you think he will now?"

"Who gives a shit?" Lena explodes. "Maybe I don't respect him. Maybe I don't even like him. Maybe I just like fucking him. Is that okay? Am I allowed to like sex? If we're both cool with the terms, what difference does it make? Do you deeply respect everyone you've fucked?"

"That's not the point," Darren says stiffly.

"No, the point is neither of us should give the other shit about their romantic choices."

"This isn't about me! You always do this!"

"Why don't you just hook up with that James kid and get off my back already?"

Darren blinks. "James? What . . . why would you . . ."

"You've been giving each other doe eyes since we started working there."

"Not even!"

"Oh, totally."

"He's not even . . ."

"What?"

"He's . . . whatever . . . African. Or from Senegal, I mean."

Lena stares dumbfounded at him. "What the *hell* does that mean?"

Darren actually shudders. "No! I don't mean . . . *that*! I don't . . . I just mean . . . he's all whatever, religious. Like they are. I guess. I don't know."

Lena rubs her forehead as if there's a deep ache between her temples.

"Darren . . . *you* were baptized Roman Catholic."

"I know that. Look. James isn't even . . . he's not . . ."

"Jesus. *Gay*, Darren. The word is *gay*. You're gay. You're a gay dude. You're allowed to say it."

"Don't fucking tell me what I am!"

"I've been telling you what you are since we were sixteen and if I didn't you wouldn't be able to admit it to yourself!"

"Yeah, you're so damn smart. If you're so smart why are you screwing your boss who's also a colossal asshole who you hate?"

Lena slams her coffee mug down on the bar top.

"I think a far more rational question would be, 'Why am I working at a fucking catering company in Long Island City where you either get turned into monsters or mauled by them at every single damn event?' Oh, wait! I know! Because *you* wouldn't leave when we had the chance and I had to stay to watch your ass! Like always!"

She storms across the living room and down the hall

to her bedroom.

"I didn't see you not cashing that fat paycheck last week!" he yells after her.

Her response is a slammed door.

"Bitch," Darren mutters to himself, and immediately feels bad for saying it.

STAFF MEETING

Rare is the occasion the majority of Sin du Jour's employees find themselves in the same room at the same time.

"I forgot we even had a conference room," Dorsky remarks.

The other chefs laugh, spearheaded by Rollo, ever Dorsky's Eastern Bloc sidekick in the kitchen. Darren joins in because he finally seems to have been accepted by the rest of the line.

Nikki doesn't laugh because it's not funny.

Lena doesn't laugh because it's not funny and she's pissed off at Darren. She makes it a point to stare at him, calling out his courtesy laugh with her eyes.

The kitchen staff is seated around the hand-carved mahogany table in the middle of the room. Dorsky sits at one end of the table, Rollo to his right, Chevet and Tenryu to his left like some sort of pseudo–lion pride arrangement.

Darren sits next to James, who he isn't trying to ignore but can't seem to bring himself to acknowledge.

Lena and Nikki are slightly removed from the others,

Nikki quietly explaining some esoteric vintage hair-styling technique Lena will never understand, let alone attempt to implement.

The Stocking & Receiving Department fills chairs lining the wall in the back of the room. Hara has to sit on two seats pushed together, and even then they seem inadequate. Beside him Ritter and Cindy are trading fluid, half-speed hand strikes they take turns throwing and blocking, practicing some form of martial arts. Moon is sunk into the corner playing a Nintendo 3DS.

Ryland, the company's resident alchemist, is crashed out on a sofa sitting alongside the conference table. He's on his eighteenth cigarette of the day and seventh glass of white wine.

Pacific and Mr. Mirabel huddle against the wall on the other side of the table, sharing the earbuds jacked into Pacific's digital music player.

They're all waiting on Bronko and Jett. The only ones absent are Boosha, in official exile in her apothecary after inadvertently turning the staff into sex monsters, and White Horse and his granddaughter/assistant/chaperone, Little Dove.

Bronko enters the room a few minutes later, Jett following excitedly on his heels. She seems even more wired than usual, whereas lately Bronko has seemed unusually removed. He's been that way since the royal goblin wedding a month ago. He disappeared inexplicably at the end of that night. They got a memo from him to take an extended weekend, and when they all returned to work Bronko's entire demeanor and mood had changed. They rarely see him at family meals, the staff lunches and dinners they cook and share together during the long days in the kitchen. He barely leaves his office anymore. No one has yet to force a conversation about it, but there isn't a single one of them, even and especially Lena and Darren, who hasn't noticed and been inwardly disturbed by the change.

Sin du Jour's executive chef is carrying a long, rolled-up ream of glossy paper. He walks to the opposite end of the table and looms there, ignoring the chair.

"I am quite frankly shocked y'all made it in here together and on time, so thanks for that," he addresses them dryly.

Scattered, affectionate laughter fills the room.

Bronko rubs at his prickly neck. Many of them have also noticed that recently he goes abnormally longer than usual without shaving.

"I know you've all been busting hump prepping for the TaurusCon gala, but something urgent's come up and we're going to need to do a little tap dancing. I wasted a couple of weeks trying to get us out of it because frankly I think we've got enough on our plate, and I probably should've told y'all about it sooner, and that's on me, but we are where we are now and we're all just gonna have to deal with it."

He extends his arm over the table and unfurls the paper on his hand, laying it down flat on the tabletop.

It's a movie poster.

The title is *Authority over Unclean Spirits* and the one-sheet is dominated by an image of a very pretty actor the makeup department has tried very hard to make unpretty (which seems ludicrous to Lena, among others, considering how many talented ugly people there already are in the world) kneeling in the mud in front of barbed wire, looking to the sky.

"I know this one," James says. He holds up his smart phone. "I have no time for going to the movies, but I downloaded the Movie Trailers app. It is very good."

Bronko seems less than interested. "Yeah, from what I gather it's about a mentally challenged Jew during the Holocaust who's also gay or some such thing."

"So their asses just want all the Oscars," Cindy comments from the back, propping an elbow on Ritter's shoulder and resting her cheek in her palm.

"Oh, it already has intense Oscar buzz!" Jett informs her brightly, Cindy's sarcasm completely sailing over her head.

Likewise, the half-dozen expressions aimed at her

silently asking, "Who actually talks like that?" go utterly unnoticed by Jett.

"So . . . what, boss?" Dorsky asks, not getting it. "You don't want to go see it alone, or what?"

Bronko sighs, looking to Jett, who appears to be about a second away from her head popping off.

Bronko gives her a nod.

"We're doing the studio's premiere party!" Jett announces, practically vibrating.

Most of the line groans.

"A movie premiere?" Lena asks, her face slightly scrunched in a mix of confusion and disdain. "That . . . doesn't seem like Sin du Jour's mandate, unless I misunderstood you, Chef."

"Gotta say I'm with Tarr on this one, boss," Dorsky adds.

"Just this one?" Rollo asks under his breath, punctuating it with a low chuckle.

Lena looks over at him, a gunshot expression forming on her face that she quickly forces blank.

She can feel Nikki watching her suspiciously and Darren watching her judgingly.

"It seems we've developed a sudden rep in La-La Land," Bronko says. "Word on the goblin prince's wedding got out the very next damn day, it seems. Everyone in town in the know wants us. This premiere shindig is just the first request to make it past Allensworth. I guess the producers have a lot of stroke with the goblin hierarchy, and that is what we do."

Dorsky raises an eyebrow. "They all know that the wedding was a Mongolian clusterfuck that nearly killed all the guests and not a theme party, right?"

"Can they tell the difference out there?" Nikki asks so earnestly it's hard to tell she's joking.

Lena snorts.

"Look, I don't book the gigs," Bronko says irritably.

His mood isn't what takes them aback. It's his admission of powerlessness. Though they're all more or less aware Sin du Jour operates at the discretion of Allensworth and the government, it's unlike Bronko not to maintain an air of total control.

"The fact of the matter is we're gonna be in the weeds," he continues. "The movie comes out next month. The movie premiere is next Friday night."

This time the groans are louder and more contiguous.

"That's right. It's short notice and we're double-booked."

"Where are they premiering the stupid movie?" Dorsky asks. "Union Square?"

"The premiere isn't in New York. It's in Los Angeles."

Everyone who groaned is suddenly hooting and hollering.

"Oh, now it's not such a damn inconvenience."

"Settle your shit," Dorsky instructs the line, quieting them and badly suppressing his grin.

To Bronko he says: "That depends, boss. Who's going to LA?"

"Not you," Bronko says flatly.

Dorsky's grin disappears.

"I need you here running point on the convention gala. I'll head up LA. I know the people and the terrain better. The premiere party is a lot more exclusive, so thankfully we can keep the crew tight. I'll take Tarr and Vargas."

Everyone on the line who isn't Lena and Darren is incensed, and vocal about it.

Save James, who clasps Darren's shoulder and smiles at him in sincere congratulations.

Darren stiffens, forces a grin.

"Nikki, Jett needs you for a lot of what she's got planned for the party. Dorsky, y'all are doing a straight buffet line with no hors d'oeuvres service and we are; so Pac, Mo, you're on board with me too."

"Wicked!" Pacific hollers, high-fiving Mr. Mirabel.

"Oh, come on!" Dorsky yells at the ceiling. "Bong Hits McGee and the World's Oldest Man here get a free trip to the coast and we're stuck doing the half-and-half con?"

"Tag, you know 'half-and-half' is a pejorative use of an ableist term," Jett chastises. "Both the minotaur contingent *and* the centaur contingent find it highly offensive—"

"Oh-my-god-Jett-whatever," Dorsky groans. "They're a bunch of dudes with bull heads and horse bodies who have to have their annual love fest during ComicCon so no one will notice or hunt them for sport. It's bad enough we had to prepare two menus because the centaurs get all uppity about eating horse food."

"They are not horses, Tag!" Jett insists.

"Did he just say 'uppity'?" Cindy asks Ritter behind the chefs. "Did I just hear that?"

"The point is," Dorsky continues quickly, "does seniority count for nothing around here? We get the splooge line at the geeks and freaks carnival and the newbies and the pastry puff get to go surfing?"

Beside him, Rollo whistles approvingly and claps his hands.

"Goddammit, this is a job, not a vacation!" Bronko snaps at them, his irritation shifting to real anger. "Are you my sous-chef, or not?"

Dorsky is caught off guard, but he recovers, putting away his cavalier attitude.

"Yes, Chef," he says seriously.

"Then act like it. I'm leaving you in charge. You're executive chef while I'm gone. I want things here to go off without a hitch. Tarr, Vargas, you'll meet with me tomorrow on menu and pre-prep. We fly out Wednesday. We'll shop and cook onsite. Nikki, get with Jett before then. Y'all have carte blanche on dessert. Whatever you want to do."

"Oh, cool!" Nikki says. "Thanks, Chef."

In the back of the room, Ritter raises his hand.

"Yeah, Ritt?"

"What do you need my team to do?" Ritter asks.

"Oh, right. Dorsky's good and the premiere party is a mostly human, non-magicked-type menu for the most part. Take the week off. Y'all deserve it."

"Does that include me?" Ryland asks around his unfiltered cigarette. "I am an honorary member of the department, after all."

"No, you're not," Ritter and Cindy say in perfect unison.

"You're going to prepare whatever Jett and Cindy need for the goblin portion of the guest list," Bronko says.

"Typical," Ryland mutters.

"Ritter, you and yours enjoy the break."

"Then what did we need to be here for?" Moon whines.

"Boy, you are lucky I sign a paycheck for you, useful as you are most of the time," Bronko replies shortly.

Moon appears to genuinely think about it, and shrugs.

"Fair enough," he says, returning to his game.

"Pac, we'll need a few more servers, but no goddamn Craigslist this time, y'hear?" Bronko instructs him.

"No worry, boss," Pacific assures him.

"Any questions need addressing right now?" Bronko asks them.

Nobody voices one.

"All right, then."

Bronko leaves them, his stride fast and labored.

It takes most of them a moment to shake off the bad feeling in the room.

As Lena heads for the door, she finds herself meeting Ritter in the back of the room.

"Congratulations," he says to her.

Lena genuinely doesn't understand.

"On what?"

"You're moving up."

Lena half-laughs. "Right. By default."

"Take it however it comes."

Ritter grins at her, just a little.

Behind him, Cindy performs a physiological miracle by rolling her eyes without her eyes ever moving in their sockets.

Ritter turns to walk out the door of the conference

room and finds Dorsky casually blocking his way.

Dorsky is a head taller than him, forcing Ritter to look up.

Despite that, one would be hard-pressed not to choose Ritter as the more intimidating between them.

"You need something, Number Two?" he asks.

Dorsky grins down at him. "Nothing worthy of the Indiana Jones of grocery shopping, I'm sure."

"Indiana Jones was an imperialist grave-robbing sumbitch," Cindy chimes in from behind Ritter. "I hate those fucking movies."

Ritter has no readable expression or tone when he says to Dorsky, "You're in my way."

"Am I?" Dorsky asks, still grinning. "I guess I didn't notice I was in your way until just now."

"Jesus," Lena murmurs, mortified.

Then, louder: "If you two want to piss for distance do it in the men's room."

She pushes her way past them both and out the door.

Ritter and Dorsky watch her go, the sous-chef with a confused expression and the head of Stocking & Receiving with the subtlest hint of a frown.

"I like her despite myself," Cindy says quietly.

SHARED MISTAKES

"So what're you thinking for this thing?" Lena asks Nikki.

They're in the small pastry kitchen that is Nikki's sole domain and one of Lena's favorite rooms in Sin du Jour. Nikki is carefully laying Saran Wrap over trays of beautifully molded maple rum panna cotta and trays of equally beautifully molded terrines of raw bakery waste.

The former dish is dessert for the centaurs attending the annual TaurusCon gala in Manhattan.

The latter is dessert for the minotaur guests.

She's carefully labeling the top of each plastic-wrapped tray with Post-it notes.

Confusing one for the other would not only be the worst experience of any non-minotaur's life, it would probably also kill them.

"Cherries jubilee, maybe," Nikki answers her. "It's Hollywood. I figure light something on fire, right?"

"That seems kind of basic for you. I'll just say it."

Nikki grins like someone with a secret. "I'll jazz it up. What are you all doing for dinner service?"

Lena frowns. "It's all supposed to be low-cal, low-carb, everything with a vegan option."

"So? I cook vegetarian for my sister all the time. It doesn't mean you can't have fun, get inspired."

Lena shrugs. "It's not so much the health thing. Just feels like we're going all vanilla."

"Hey, what's the static between you and Darren all of a sudden?"

"He's being a judgmental little prick," Lena says quite matter-of-factly.

"About what?"

"Who I sleep with."

Nikki's eyes go wide. She had been sliding clear-wrapped trays into a fridge. She shoves the one she's holding in hastily and quickly swings the door shut, walking back over to Lena.

"Who are you—" she begins, and then stops herself. "Wait."

Nikki jogs over to a pantry, grabs a bottle of wine, a cork, two glasses, and jogs back.

She has the cork popped and the glasses filled in less than ten seconds. Nikki shoves one at Lena.

"Who are you sleeping with?" she asks.

It's an excited question, but coming from Nikki and considering the answer Lena imagines it sounds like a homicide detective interrogating her.

She frowns into her glass, hesitating.

"Look, I haven't told you this because I got the vibe you and he have history, but I'm also not willing to lie to you about it."

Nikki stares at her in sudden confusion.

"I've been hooking up with Dorsky," Lena says, sipping her wine and coughing because it goes down the wrong pipe. "Since the lockdown."

"Oh," Nikki says immediately.

And then she doesn't say anything.

Instead she drinks her wine.

Then keeps drinking it.

She keeps drinking it until her glass is empty.

"Oh," she repeats, breathless.

"So . . ." Lena struggles. "Have I broken some lady code here? Like, how pissed are you?"

"I'm not."

"You're not? Seriously? Because you don't seem okay, that's for damn sure."

"I'm surprised," Nikki says evenly. "But I can't rightly be pissed at you or judge you for making mistakes I've made myself. That would be like, super unfair."

Now it's Lena's turn to say, "Oh."

Nikki nods.

"All I'm going to say is I get it. There's an appeal there. But what I'd add is . . . that appeal has a very short reach. Especially when you work with him."

Lena holds up her hands. "I don't want to marry the dude, Nikki. It's just . . . a thing that's working for me right now."

Nikki nods. "I understand."

"So . . . we're actually cool? Like, really cool? Not false assurances and private bloodletting followed by passive-aggressive girl war cool?"

"I don't know what that means," Nikki says. "So no. I'm not mad. Really. I am worried about you, but that's because . . . you know."

"Yeah. I know. Same here."

Nikki nods again.

"Is this a bad time?" a young voice asks from the pantry kitchen entrance.

They both look over to find Little Dove standing there, unsure and seeming as though she wants to turn around and run.

Nikki works up her warmest smile. "Hey, Lill. No. You're always welcome here."

Relief visibly washes over Little Dove. "Oh, good. You just, you both looked all intense and I didn't want to be like—"

"It's cool," Lena echoes Nikki.

Little Dove slides onto a stool at the station over which they're drinking their wine.

"I just had to get away from Grandpop for a while,"

she says, smoothing her hands back through her long hair. "This is usually the part of the week where I snap a little."

"It's Tuesday," Lena says flatly.

Little Dove nods. "I know."

"So . . . bad day?" Nikki asks.

Little Dove takes a long, deep breath. "Well, let's see. I spent an hour looking for his lost blood pressure medication, only when I called the doctor he told me Grandpop stopped taking those meds a year ago, and he just forgot. Then I had to call all of my sixty-four-year-old grandfather's bookies and cancel the bets he makes every week behind my back. Then when I told him to stop doing that for the fifty millionth time we fought for another two hours."

"Jesus," Lena says.

"Yeah. He's . . . he really is a brilliant man, in his way. And he loves me. Again, in his way. But if I wanted to spend my life as a babysitter I'd prefer actual real babies. But we'd never make this kind of money anywhere else."

Lena and Nikki both nod with genuine empathy at that last statement.

Lena in particular feels the girl's pain.

She takes up the bottle Nikki opened and pours Little Dove a glass.

"Oh, Lena," Nikki waves her hands. "I don't think

she's—" She looks at Little Dove. "How old are you again, Lill?"

"She's old enough even if she isn't old enough," Lena insists.

Little Dove grins at that, taking the glass gratefully.

Lena clinks her own against it.

They drink.

"So what *do* you want to do, Lill?" Nikki asks.

She shrugs. "I don't know, really. Do you like baking?"

Nikki smiles. "It's like therapy they pay me to have."

"I feel that way about eating what she bakes," Lena adds.

Little Dove laughs, then a serious expression overtakes it.

"Could you . . . like, teach me? Maybe?"

Nikki stares at her, genuinely taken aback.

But she couldn't be happier if the girl had asked Nikki to teach her how to do victory rolls with her hair.

"Absolutely," she tells Little Dove, sincerely.

"You know, nobody ever asked me what I wanted to do before," Little Dove says.

She seems at once rueful and appreciative.

"Well, you're one up on me," Lena assures her. "Nobody has yet."

"You figured it out, though," Nikki reminds her.

Lena laughs, downing the rest of her wine and replacing the glass on the countertop a little too hard.

She stares up at the bright overhead kitchen lights.

"Have I?" she asks no one in particular. "Have I really?"

PRE-PRODUCTION

"Didn't we option this one's spec?" Producer One asks Producer Two, using his Italian-loafered foot to prod the eviscerated writer in question.

There's a whole pile of them.

Dead writers, that is.

Most of their hearts have been ripped from their chests. Some of them are missing their brains. Several are still clutching screenplays in their arms.

"The only screenwriter whose name I remember is Chayefsky."

"Because he's the only writer to ever get the 'film by' credit?"

"No, because he skull-fucked that harpy in front of everyone at Nicholson's party that time."

"Oh yeah. The party where Nicholson passed out all that great old-school biker acid?"

"Yep."

"Classic."

The bodies are stacked high near the door of a windowless conference room. A long-deceased Warner brother is currently devouring the heart of the writer Producer Two can't remember. He sits eternally at the head of a granite slab conference table surrounded by all the big old-time Hollywood moguls.

They're not zombies, strictly speaking.

They don't need to eat human organs to survive.

They just demand them.

In truth no one living knows what they are anymore, but since the 1950s they've sat here in their best funereal suits, eyeballs black and flesh necrotic but never rotting off. They don't move from their chairs. They don't speak.

They just eat.

All day.

Every day.

The major studios in town take turns supplying them daily with fresh writers, their overwhelming preference. No one in Hollywood knows what will happen if they stop feeding the moguls. But no one wants to find out. On the whole it's become little more than a fad religion for the elite, not unlike Scientology, albeit far more secretive and exclusive. Feeding the moguls and paying them homage and seeking blessings for your film is the ultimate status symbol in the most private and powerful quarters of the industry.

Producer One and Producer Two wait patiently by the door as the head of a studio currently scoring big adapting dystopian novels for "young adults" (code around town for books written by middle-aged authors who've failed at every other genre writing for adults, all of whom have nothing but contempt for teenagers) into big-budget movies makes an offering to the moguls for the success of his newest franchise.

He places the brain of the author upon whose dystopian YA books the franchise will be based.

Producer One recalls reading that the third book has yet to be written.

He idly muses whether the lack of a brain will make a difference in the quality of the writing.

"Did you hear that shit about the ACLU coming to town to 'investigate' the industry's hiring practices?" Producer One asks while they wait.

"No," Producer Two says. "What about them?"

"They're 'gendered' or whatever the bleeding-heart word is. Apparently less than ten percent of all writers and directors are women."

"We can't get it any lower than that," Producer Two complains. "A few are bound to slip through now and then. It's not a foolproof system."

"No, they're saying it should be more."

"Oh." It still takes a moment for the realization to fully sink in. "*Oh!* Fuck them."

"I know, right? It's exhausting enough spending all

day pretending to care about gays and minorities, now I have to fire some idiot I know we can control with some bitch who won't listen to us?"

He's quiet a moment, then: "ACLU. Investigation. My bleached asshole. Who do they think they are, Philip Marlowe? What're they gonna do, send me a sternly worded email? Write an op-ed in *LA Magazine*? Fuck 'em."

Producer Two flicks her chin at the conference table. "Makes you long for their day," she says.

Producer One frowns. "These fossils?" he says in the most hushed of voices. "Please. We're answering to a higher power now."

"No joke," she agrees.

They both duck as necrotic Irving Thalberg, the original "Boy Wonder" Hollywood mogul, angrily hurls the brain offered by the studio head across the room. It hits the wall behind them with a sickening "splat."

Producer One shakes his head as the studio boss scurries past, disappearing through the doors leading out of the conference room in shame and fear.

"Never bring them book authors."

"Let alone a 'sci-fi' author," Producer Two says, flabbergasted. "What was he thinking?"

"Fuck him. We're up."

A ghoulish attendant beckons them both to the vacant end of the conference table.

The producers approach it with what they hope looks like reverence.

Producer Two raises her arms ceremonially. "Our film is *Authority over Unclean Spirits.*"

Producer One holds aloft a small ornate box as an offering.

"The ashes of a thousand film and television bloggers!" he announces grandly.

A murmured wave of interest and approval passes around the table of undead moguls.

Producer One places the box on the tabletop.

Producer Two hands him a decades-old, out-of-circulation thousand-dollar bill rolled into a tight cylinder.

He places it gingerly atop the box and slides it down the long length of the table.

Jack Warner stops it with a slap of his gray-black, craggy hand. He pinches the G-note awkwardly between two dead fingertips and gruffly flips open the lid of the box.

The mogul snorts half a gram of the mixed ashes inside through the rolled-up bill and then his left nostril. His black pool eyes roll back in his rotted head, which tilts into the plush leather of his chair's headrest as euphoria rushes through his decaying form.

The producers smile at each other.

"Jackpot," Producer One silently mouths.

A few minutes later they're trekking down the stairs of the famous landmark studio water tower inside which the mogul's conference room temple is hidden.

"So we're all set for the premiere party, yes?" Producer One asks. "We've got a helluva lot more riding on it than on that bullshit back in there."

"We're locked and loaded," she assures him. "Their party planner used to be hot shit out here years back, I guess. Before a half-dozen guests died at one of her events. She couldn't get arrested after that. Anyway, she's frothing at the mouth to do an industry party again. I couldn't shut her up."

"Sweet. That should make things easier."

"Did you ever eat at any of Luck's restaurants back in the day?" Producer Two asks.

"Nope. Met him a couple times when he was out here, saw that show he had. His food any good?"

"Oh, epic. I'm stoked we're not killing them all till after dinner."

THE BEST TACO TRUCK IN LA

There's no truck, to begin with.

Bronko instructed them all not to eat on the plane (that wasn't much of a chore). He also told them to skip dinner at the downtown Roosevelt Hotel, where the studio is housing them, because he'd be taking them all out for the best late supper in the city of Los Angeles.

Considering the food city LA has become, and the hook-ups Bronko has reportedly retained from the height of his celebrity chef stardom, it filled them all with a sense of wonder and anticipation that's become a real physical acid bubbling in their stomachs as the hour approaches.

Lena, Darren, and Nikki traded many guesses about which five-star restaurant in whose kitchen Bronko had no doubt secured them all a chef's table and special tasting menu. Would it be a classic Hollywood standard like Wolfgang Puck's Spago in Beverly Hills? Or would it be a newer fine-dining institution like Mélisse or Chef Michael Cimarusti's Michelin star–winning Providence?

A little after nine o'clock in the evening Bronko drives

them south on the 101 from their hotel in a rented SUV. Jett was forced to abstain (too much to do, she insisted with the fervency of a hamster on meth), but Lena, Darren, Nikki, Pacific, and Mr. Mirabel weren't about to miss the festivities.

They exit on Caesar Chavez Avenue, and it isn't five minutes before he pulls over and parks at the curb.

Their minds cloud with confusion and their hearts and stomachs drop.

It looks like a good place to buy heroin and the worst place to look for a good meal.

Running up against the end of a chain-link fence in an empty blacktop lot, the taco "stand" looks more like a taco truck was turned upside-down and its contents shaken loose. There's no signage of any kind. In fact, there's no construction of any kind. Several folding plastic tables of assorted sizes are jammed up against each other to form the prep, cooking, and serving counters. String lights from a hardware store woven in the fence and hung overhead light the corner. There are a dozen large plastic coolers visible under the folding tables.

An eclectic crowd has gathered near the otherwise barren-looking street corner. There are several Harley-Davidson motorcycles leaning to one side at the curb next to the newest-model Porsche upon which several of the hipster elite are lounging with their tacos. Late-night workers in coveralls stand about grabbing a quick, cherished bite before their shifts begin. A few neighborhood kids chase a ball through the scene, being yelled at by diners in mismatched lawn chairs sitting on the sidewalk.

"Everybody queue up," Bronko instructs them as they file out of the rental car. "You're all getting one of everything, and I don't want to see any returns."

The cooks look at each other, unsure.

"Have they been inspected, Chef?" Nikki asks, suspicious.

"Don't know, don't care," Bronko replies simply. "Line up! It's all on me!"

The five of them comply, stepping up onto the sidewalk and lining up in front of the makeshift stand.

A cauldron-sized pot is simmering at the end of the folding table facing the street, being stirred diligently by a twentysomething Mexican woman in a stained apron.

When the smell of the conjoining spices and cooking meat hits their nostrils there isn't a one of them who retains a single doubt something special is about to happen.

"Christ, look at that," Lena marvels, pointing.

Half a dozen kinds of maddeningly aromatic taco fillings are being scooped from as many small serving dishes arranged on the table near the large pot.

There's carne asada, carnitas, al pastor, cabeza (delicious shredded beef cheek), and even tripe and crispy white fish.

"I take it back," Nikki says readily, suddenly starving and eager to satiate herself.

For a scant one dollar apiece an older woman who may be the pot-stirrer's mother or grandmother places ready-made tortillas the size of saucers on a paper plate and covers each with a different filling, serving them all one of each kind, then directing them to another table alongside their modular empire upon which all manner of communal condiments are waiting, along with napkins and an ice chest filled with cans of soda and bottles of water.

They all ladle their preferred levels of homemade salsa verde and fresh-cut jalapeños onto their tacos and start eating.

The experience is more transcendent than anything you'll find in a Michelin-starred kitchen.

Anything.

"Don't get me wrong, you can still find damn good taco trucks all around LA," Bronko explains around a mouthful of succulent carnitas. "But a few years back the city legislated a lot of the independents out of business. And with the food truck boom a lot of corporate outfits and high-end start-ups moved in. Now it's easier to find lobster and truffle-oil popcorn out of a truck than a damn taco, let alone a good one."

Bronko, with nothing resembling grace or self-consciousness, jams the rest of the heaven-filled tortilla in his mouth, chews with relish, and gulps it down.

"If you want the legit shit," he pronounces in its wake, "this is where you go."

"It's amazing," Nikki says.

"I couldn't make these," Lena admits, genuinely in awe. "I can't even—"

Whatever she was about to say becomes a deep belch.

She doesn't seem to care, and it does not impede her next bite in any way.

"What about the Kogi truck?" Darren asks. "They're pretty good."

Bronko's eyes seem to have forgotten the question before Darren is done asking it, their attention returning to the counter, but his right hand responds by simulating masturbation.

Darren flusters.

"Who's ready for a second round?" Bronko asks the chefs, the servers, as well as everyone else milling about the open-air taco restaurant.

Lena, Darren, and Nikki all exchange cautious smiles. It's the happiest they've seen Bronko in weeks, but more than that, it's the first time in those weeks he's behaved more like the chef they've come to know, trust, and follow.

Bronko buys every patron waiting several more tacos.

The Sin du Jour crew spends another hour devouring the handheld treats, discussing and arguing which ones are their personal favorites and why.

Not a single one of them gives another thought to fine-dining restaurants or haute cuisine.

When their bellies are bulging and their eyes can barely stay open under the influence of a threatening food coma, Bronko leads them back to the rented SUV.

Before he does, he leans over the main table of the open-air kitchen and slips the older woman several hundred-dollar bills with his whispered compliments.

They all climb back inside the rental car with great effort, Lena sitting in the front seat beside Bronko.

"If you should ever find yourself in charge of a kitchen like ours, Tarr," he says to her quite sagely, "I want you to take a lesson from this."

"Which is what, Chef?" she asks, her guard brought all the way down by food overload.

"When you're in the weeds and staring down the barrel of a teeming mama-jama of a gig"—he jerks a thumb at the window, in the direction of the taco stand—"that there is how you pre-game."

Lena smiles openly at him, and for perhaps only the second time she's truly glad she's part of Bronko's crew.

"Who wants dessert?" Bronko asks the rest of them. "I know a place."

The chorus of groans and protests from the back of the SUV is deafening.

WEARY STRANGERS IN A
SAVAGE LAND

Lena finds herself feeling oddly exposed by cooking in a kitchen that's not nestled in the brick fortress of Sin du Jour. She realizes she's come to view what they do with a deep, foreboding secrecy, and violating that secrecy actually filled her with a quiet panic for the first few hours in their temporary workspace.

The morning after their truckless taco excursion and the inevitable ensuing epic bathroom-sitting session that followed (Lena had time to read an entire Kameron Hurley essay), they were shuttled to an entirely different hotel to begin working on the premiere party menu. The hotel that the movie studio has booked for the party is much larger and newer than the Roosevelt, where the Sin du Jour crew is holed up.

Bronko, Lena, and Darren spent yesterday shopping and prepping what ingredients they could without sacrificing the quality and freshness of the dishes they have planned. Today they're bunkered in one of the hotel's kitchens, cooking.

Lena hasn't seen Nikki since the night they arrived. Nikki and Jett are sequestered in another wing of the hotel, presumably preparing whatever dessert showpiece Jett needs Nikki to execute.

Neither of them would tell the others what they had in mind.

Pacific and Mr. Mirabel are supposedly interviewing temporary servers, and no doubt smoking a large amount of weed in between or possibly during that process.

Lena is sautéing piles of expertly broken-down Belgian endive in several large pans while Darren dices fresh ingredients for the smoothie bar they have planned for the premiere party.

They're making it a point to ignore each other.

Every now and then Lena glances over at Bronko, towering over his own station as he forms a mixture of squash, quinoa, and spices into perfectly uniform patties, frying them into fritters.

She can't help watching his impossibly large hands perform delicate cooking tasks.

He still seems to her like a contradiction, almost a figure from another age, as if he should be in some secluded forest that time and civilization has forgotten, cutting down trees with an axe.

"You two're awful quiet," Bronko suddenly informs them, although his tone doesn't say he feels one way or another about this fact.

Neither Lena nor Darren answers at first.

Instead they glance at each other and back to their stations at different times.

Lena finally says, "No offense, Chef, but you're not exactly doing stand-up either."

"Yeah, but I know why I'm being quiet. I want to know what's up with the two of you. You on the outs or something? I thought you weren't a couple?"

"We're not," Lena reiterates.

Darren remains silent.

"So? What, then? Roommate thing? One of you leaves dishes in the sink, the other's a clean freak? What?"

"It's not kitchen business, Chef," Lena says.

Bronko nods. "You know, that's fair enough. Ordinarily I'd agree with you. When I ran the kitchens in my restaurants back in the day, I didn't never want to hear anyone's personal business. No room for it on my line, I thought."

Lena just nods, glad the matter seems to be settled.

However, Bronko isn't done: "Thing is, Sin du Jour ain't that. It's not like any other line in any other kitchen in any overpriced, overhyped piles of potato hay and squirts of tomato water horseshit nouveau eatin' house. We're different. We have to be. We're cooks, yeah. That's our job. But our world isn't the restaurant world. It's dangerous. It's real. And the chef on the line next to you is more than a cook, they're watching your back and you're watching theirs in that big, bad, dangerous world. We're all each other has. And that means there's no room for petty squabbles. Having been a soldier, Tarr, I'd expect you of all people to understand that."

Bronko says all of this without much emotion in his voice, and the bizarre matter-of-factness somehow makes it more powerful for Lena and Darren.

Their executive chef takes his current pan off its heat and picks up a kitchen towel. He wipes off his hands, moving away from his station and momentarily exiting the kitchen.

"He's right, you know," Darren says a little while later as he mixes up batches of savory and sweet creams for the smoothies bar.

"Of course he's right," Lena shoots back at him, also not taking her eyes off her work. "Doesn't make me any less pissed."

Darren's lips tighten. "Fine. Let me know when you're over it."

Lena expertly flips the vegetables in one of her pans through the air in a perfect arc, the flames beneath the pan rising for one brief, incendiary moment.

"Will do," she says.

OSTER

How Ritter ends up bashing in the Easter Bunny's skull with a sledgehammer is a funny story.

He bought the converted brick townhouse on East 105th Street a year ago. Ritter chose central Canarsie in Brooklyn because it remains one of the least gentrified neighborhoods in the entire city. Ritter wasn't born a New Yorker, but it hasn't left him any less disgusted as he bears witness to one of the most unique, rooted, and diverse collectives in America devoured by the rich and steadily conforming to some grotesquely overpriced hipster Disneyland ideal.

The townhouse had been divided into two rental units long ago and was falling apart when Ritter bought the place for a song. He's spent the majority of his downtime since then fixing it up, and it is finally coming into focus as a home; for Ritter, the first real home he's ever known.

The night of the premiere party, Ritter, like the rest of the Stocking & Receiving Department, is enjoying some much needed rest and relaxation in the sanctuary of their separate domiciles around the city. Ritter spends several hours lounging on the Stressless Ambassador recliner in his living room, sipping Puerto Rican rum and half-watching *The Man from Nowhere* on his modest television.

Earlier in the day he finally began knocking down the wall between rental units with the end goal of turning the first floor into a single space. There's an eight-by-six gap smashed through the raw brick. Ritter laid down plastic sheeting on both sides of it. From his chair he can glimpse the edge of the wheelbarrow in the other unit filled with the resulting rubble, a dust-covered sledgehammer resting atop the pile. It was backbreaking work, and he's still feeling the effects.

Ritter takes down his third finger of rum, ingesting the climactic fight scene of the South Korean noir thriller like other people listen to an inspiring poetry recital. The chief henchman character, played by Thai actor Thanayong Wongtrakul, charges at the movie's hero with a karambit. The titular man from nowhere, played by Bin Won, defends with a short, straight blade. The ensuing knife duel is one of Ritter's favorite action scenes. Like most great movie fights, he finds, it's grounded in solid real-world principal and theory while being too fluid and cooperative to ever be a real fight.

Still, the quick, expert motions are hypnotic and charged to watch.

As the action on-screen wanes, Ritter's gaze falls to one side of the TV screen. Ritter has populated his home with few personal touches and many expensive amenities to help him recoup after dangerous, physically taxing work. The only real decoration in the space is an expansive framed movie poster on the wall behind him. It's an original bus stop advertisement for the 1971 film *Billy Jack,* the movie that introduced Ritter to the martial art hapkido.

The most personal touches in the townhouse, however, are the framed photographs arranged on the television stand. Ritter is in each one with the same three men. They're all in their twenties, as physically fit as they'd ever be.

In one of the photographs they're all clad in jungle camo BDUs, posing at the base of a mountain in Michoacan. There's Migs, cradling an experimental thermite grenade launcher, face plastered with a shit-eating grin. Banquo stands in the background, more serious, a machete sheathed on either hip. The man next to Ritter is a slightly younger version of him, his brother, Marcus. Ritter always appears the nondescript, everyman version standing beside his brother, who always had an edge about him, a darkness that radiated mostly in his eyes.

They were freelancing off the books for the DEA at the time, exterminating the powerful *brujos* working for the drug cartels. In their downtime they'd hunt harpies in the mountain ranges and raze the odd illegal logging camp, enjoying the favor of the local villages and towns the loggers terrorized either for kicks or for the sake of their operation.

In the photograph beside it they're all piled into a natural hot springs in Vilcabamba, holding bottles of the pilsner beer brewed in Ecuador and roughhousing with each other, their very real laughter frozen in time on celluloid.

That was the last good time, before they were all loaned out to Allensworth's Witchcraft Enforcement Team initiative and they went from hunting monsters to becoming monsters.

Ritter feels the easy tears of drunkenness prick his eyes, sniffs deeply to head them off at the pass.

He decides he's drunk more than he meant to and needs to sweat it out.

He kills the TV, sets his empty tumbler aside, and stands from the recliner with a mock-groan of protest.

He built a walk-in sauna in one of the spare rooms for which he has no other use. Ten minutes later he sits naked on the lone bench, head hung with an ice-cold towel draped over it, breathing deeply and evenly.

There's a heating element filled with natural stones beside him, along with a bucket of water and a traditional ladle.

Ritter glances briefly through the clear pane of the sauna's small door at the blank wall beyond, thinking maybe he should hang something there, a painting or a poster or something.

He turns his attention to the heater, taking up the ladle and pouring water over the stones, relishing the spirits of steam that rise anew from them.

The next time he glances up the glass door in front of him has been completely overtaken by a thick veneer of steam.

However, he can still read the outline of the towering figure now standing on the other side of the glass.

Ritter blinks away the sweat running around the corners of his eyes and shakes his head, squinting at the impossibly tall outline.

It's definitely a body.

For a brief moment he thinks it must be Hara; no other human being he's ever met is that tall. However, the frame is far too slender and its shoulders too narrow.

More than that, however, is the fact this figure also has two large, protruding, distinctly rabbitlike ears hanging from its massive cranium.

Ritter immediately reaches over the pile of hot stones at his side. There are two rocks resting on the very top, one on each side of the pile that are slightly different in color and inexplicably cool to the touch.

He picks them up, one in each hand, and abruptly slams them together in front of him with a loud, grating "clack."

The effect is immediate and energetic.

An all-encompassing deep blue pall immediately overtakes the lights in the room and the rooms beyond.

It's far more than just a change in lighting, however. The air ripples, and even after it settles everything seems slightly askew, as if reality itself has just been shifted the scantest millimeter from the norm to something else.

Ritter drops the stones back in the heater and pulls the wet towel from over his head.

He rolls it up and wraps one end around his right fist, his other hand twisting its remaining length into something like a crude whip.

He stares into the glass door. The blue pall has made the outline of the figure standing on the other side much harder to make out past the steam.

"You can walk out of here right now," Ritter calls out in a casual, but hard-edged voice. "That'd be my preference. If you stay, I don't like your odds of success. This is unfamiliar terrain for you, and if you're wondering what these floodlights indicate, any magicks you may have brought along in aid of your purpose have just been rendered inert."

There's no response from beyond the glass.

Ritter sighs, slowly rising from the bench, towel-wrapped fist cocked at his hip.

He walks forward three steps and reaches out to the door handle with his other hand, gripping it firmly.

His stance spreads, feet squared back and aligned with his shoulders.

"A guy can't even have a night to himself anymore," he mutters.

Ritter yanks open the door, towel hand raised.

There's nothing waiting on the other side.

He peers cautiously into the room beyond.

Nothing.

Ritter walks out of the sauna, opening the door to the room with equal caution and still encountering no one.

He clears the hallway beyond with the precision and skill of a military assault team member, armed with a towel instead of a rifle.

Still nothing.

He reaches the end of the hallway that opens into the main living area.

The space looks barren, everything in its place.

Ritter rests his fists against his bare hips and furrows his brow, truly considering for the first time in his life that every unnatural thing he's seen and done are coming together to fuck with his perception of a perfectly normal, harmless world.

Then an Easter egg filled with spiders hits him in the face.

It breaks open on impact, releasing a skittering battalion of eight-legged arachnids that all seem to double and then triple in size once freed from the confines of the otherwise ordinary-seeming chicken egg.

Ritter immediately swipes several times at his own face with the towel whip he fashioned to fight intruders. It hurts, but it prevents the creatures from biting into his skull.

It doesn't, however, prevent the ones that have skittered down his torso from clamping their tiny fangs into his flesh half a dozen times.

The pain is sharp and localized. Ritter ignores it, his attention solely on sweeping spiders from him to the floor and stomping them with his bare feet. He kills almost a dozen within seconds, and the rest take the hint and scurry off into the corners of the room or under the welcoming darkness of the furniture.

Ritter grasps at the phantom feeling that lingers after having the surface of one's skin invaded by an insect, but there's nothing there. He's shed them all.

The damage, however, has been done.

The several bites he's sustained now feel as though he's been injected with hardening cement. It's painful, but it's nothing compared to the feeling of the venom with which he's been injected coursing through his body. In seconds he's lost feeling below his waist, and he drops to his knees before falling to his side.

Ritter manages to roll onto his back. It feels as though a splintered tree is growing inside him, its branches pushing into his every organ and appendage.

The pain is excruciating and very nearly paralyzing now.

Through its thickening haze over his vision, Ritter looks up and sees the Easter Bunny standing over him.

Oh, it's the real deal. There's no question. It's not a human being in a furry bunny costume, it is a literal anthropomorphic rabbit, and as such, rather than being cute and welcoming, it's horrifying to look at. Even more so because it's smiling down at him. As Ritter lies there, incapacitated, the corners of his eyes catch the skittering of dozens and dozens of spider legs carrying the creatures back to their master. They crawl up the rabbit's legs, idling there menacingly.

The Easter Bunny's right arm is crooked under the handle of a basket filled to a peak with brightly painted eggs, just like the one that's about to kill Ritter.

It raises its other arm and waves at him with one fingerless paw.

All things considered, it's pretty much living the

worst nightmare anyone ever had as a child.

Ritter uses his shoulders, rolling them back in succession to inch himself across the floor of the living room.

The Easter Bunny doesn't pursue him, it merely watches with head-cocked curiosity, the smile never leaving its warped face.

Ritter rolls his eyes back to find his recliner.

It's seven feet away, which might as well be a mile.

He's managed to close the gap by half when his shoulders finally give out.

He'll go no further.

Ritter focuses every ounce of will and physical strength he has left into his right arm, the one with the wet towel still clotted around his fist.

He swings his arm and by proxy the twisted length of towel at the handle on the recliner.

It's not the factory handle, however.

It's the handle he installed himself.

It takes three swings, but the third knocks it firmly 180 degrees to the right.

The seat of the recliner flips up like a lid.

Several spring-loaded objects fly up and out from the darkness beneath.

They land, scattered, on the floor near Ritter.

He sheds the towel from his hand with great effort and gropes for one of them, an ornate athame dagger, bringing it, trembling, to his chest and laying it there.

The next object he gropes for on the floor is, coincidentally, an egg-shaped container. It's bright green and emblazoned with the image of Fènghuáng, the Chinese phoenix.

Ritter forms a loose fist, the best fist he can make at the moment, around it and quickly smashes it on the floor.

An iridescent jade liquid bleeds out from inside, forming a thick pool.

Ritter retrieves the athame and presses the flat of the blade into the liquid, flipping it to the other side and repeating the action.

He can't feel his hand anymore, but it's obeying his commands nonetheless.

He spares a look across the room at the Easter Bunny.

It's still watching him with that curious body language, perhaps thinking he's about to mount some futile last-gasp counterattack.

Instead, Ritter very deliberately stabs himself in the chest with the dagger.

A knife severing his aorta should render him unconscious instantly and kill him seconds later.

Instead Ritter suddenly exhales and inhales as if he's a drowning man who's just broken above the surface of the ocean.

The effects of the spiders' venom in his system immediately slow. Sensation spreads from his heart to the rest of his body. The pain and stiffness subside, and even the spider bites release their vicelike grip on his flesh and shrink.

Ritter pulls the dagger's blade from his chest cavity.

The wound doesn't close because the blade doesn't seem to have left any wound at all.

He casts away the dagger and sits up on the floor, panting, his entire body soaked in sweat.

He stares at the Easter Bunny with hate-filled eyes that expose an inferno within him few of his team and none of their Sin du Jour coworkers have ever seen.

"I am going to kill the fuck out of you now," he informs the Easter Bunny.

In response, the creature reaches in its basket and removes an egg painted in horizontal stripes of orange and yellow.

The Easter Bunny winds up his throwing arm and chucks it at Ritter.

Ritter rolls hard to his right, moving from its path. He's back to his feet by the time the egg breaks apart against the floor, unleashing a magical burst of flame.

The flame takes immediate shape. It looks like a mandrake root made of fire, complete with a tiny mouth that immediately cackles at him in a high-pitched tone.

Then the small, grotesque elemental hurls a tangerine-sized ball of flame at him.

Ritter dives into his kitchen, behind the granite-topped island.

The fireball whizzes past the spot where Ritter was standing and lights up the curtains of a far window.

The elemental skitters from the living room toward the kitchen, hurling more fireballs as it runs past the cover of the island where Ritter is hiding.

Ritter presses himself against the lower cabinets beside the refrigerator, match-head-sized flame flittering all around him. He looks over and sees the elemental bound into sight.

Ritter reaches up and flings open the refrigerator door, its stainless-steel surface repelling the next volley of fireballs the thing unleashes.

At the same time, Ritter reaches inside the fridge past an ordinary plastic milk container from the corner store and grasps another, half-full old-fashioned glass milk bottle that belongs in a Norman Rockwell rendering.

He immediately chugs its contents, holding the liquid in his cheeks and waiting for the sound of the next crackling fireball.

After it's hurled at the refrigerator door, Ritter slams the door shut, looking down on the elemental as it winds up another incendiary pitch.

What Ritter spits at the magical pyromaniac isn't milk.

It looks more like a miniature snowstorm.

The effect blasts the elemental, freezing it solid in less than two seconds.

Ritter rises, smacking his lips compulsively, his features twisted in distaste.

He punts the sudden ice sculpture across the room with his bare foot.

It shatters against the far wall.

Ritter looks over at the Easter Bunny.

The creature is reaching into his basket for another egg.

Ritter doesn't reach for another magical weapon. He grabs the butcher knife from a nearby block and throws it with near-ninety-mile-an-hour force at the deranged hare.

The knife buries four inches of its blade in the Easter Bunny's chest.

The Bunny releases the egg it was reaching for.

It stares down at the knife protruding from its body.

It looks up at Ritter.

That damn disturbing smile never leaves its face.

In one smooth motion the Easter Bunny yanks the butcher knife from its chest cavity and hurls it back at Ritter.

He ducks a microsecond before it flies overhead, impacting an upper kitchen cabinet like a bomb, destroying it and raining lacquered wood and glass shards down over Ritter.

He turns and flees the kitchen just before another egg breaks against the refrigerator, this one filled with a searing, sizzling acid that immediately begins melting the hulking subzero and all its contents into a sparking, foul-smelling mass.

Ritter runs across the house, more eggs flying after him and narrowly missing their target.

One of them turns a large portion of wall into a patch of tall grass growing large, cartoon-looking pastel purple and yellow daisies.

Another egg shatters and disperses rusty nails in every direction, several of them catching Ritter in the back of the thigh and hip.

Ritter stumbles and curses, but he keeps running, his course taking him toward the large hole he's battered open between apartment unit walls.

He ducks through it and disappears from the Easter Bunny's sight.

The creature is forced to pursue him, holding yet another brightly colored Easter egg at the ready.

The Bunny approaches the hole in the wall, smiling as it creeps forward slowly and methodically.

It pauses in front of the jagged-edged maw between rooms.

The Easter Bunny tosses its egg just past that threshold.

It breaks open against the floor on the other side of the wall, releasing a large, noxious cloud of purple gas.

The Easter Bunny waits.

There's no sound from the other side of the hole.

No coughing, no screaming, nor the sound of a body fleeing or hitting the floor.

Satisfied, the Easter Bunny ducks its giant-eared head to pass through the hole in the wall.

Which is when Ritter finally bashes the smile from its face with a sledgehammer.

The force of the blow knocks the Easter Bunny back through the hole and off its feet.

It sounds like a felled tree hitting the forest floor when the Bunny lands.

Its lower jaw is now a hanging, lopsided thing speckled with broken teeth and dripping saliva from a permanently gaping mouth that makes the creature look utterly surprised.

Ritter emerges from the other side, the haft of the sledgehammer clutched in both hands and a faded bandanna tied around his nose and mouth.

The Easter Bunny immediately sits up, reaching for

the interior of its basket, but Ritter swings the hammer into its face again and knocks the creature prone again.

He uses the head of the sledgehammer like a shuffle-board tang to gingerly slide the basket across the floor, far away from the Bunny, without breaking any of the eggs inside.

Meanwhile, the Easter Bunny is attempting to sit up once more, but its face being more or less completely caved in seems to be impeding the process.

Ritter hampers it further by raising the sledgeham-mer high above his head and bringing it down on the Easter Bunny's cranium with as much force as he's capa-ble of imbuing the strike.

Then he does it again.

In fact, he does it until there's nothing above the Easter Bunny's shoulders but a heap of black goo sprin-kled with some fur and a detached set of oversized rabbit ears.

Finally satisfied, a panting Ritter drops the stained, dripping head of the sledgehammer to the floor and re-leases his grip on its haft.

He pulls the bandanna from his face and stands there, naked and sweating and bleeding, breathing deeply the now-untainted air.

In the last ten minutes he's been bitten, singed, poi-soned, punctured, gassed, chased, and cut up.

He's also just killed the Easter Bunny.

Needless to say, Ritter needs a moment.

Unfortunately, time is not a luxury he can afford, for several reasons.

The first of those reasons is that half his home is on fire, melting, growing unnatural shrubbery, or becoming a nest for killer spiders.

Ritter yanks nails from several parts of his body, grunting and releasing a thin stream of blood each time. He walks across his living room and down a short flight of stairs to a small coat closet in the foyer.

He opens it, reaching inside and up over the top of the frame to where an ancient serpentine bust of the god Ananke has been bolted directly to the wall.

Beside it in the darkness, a small, nondescript stone talisman hangs from a hook on a chain.

Ritter removes the talisman and loops the chain around his neck. He then reaches back up and feels for the tiny rotating sections of the snake god's stone body and begins turning them in a sequence he knows by heart.

When he's finished turning the last one there's the sudden rush of something that sounds like wind yet feels more like electricity moving through your body.

Inside the small converted townhouse in Canarsie, time literally stops.

Everything freezes in place.

Fire ceases to crackle and spread.

Acid ceases to melt.

Spiders cease their scurrying.

Everything is frozen in place except for Ritter, protected by the talisman around his neck.

He limps back upstairs, ignoring the damage done by the eggs and the fire elemental for the time being. Ananke's spell will keep them all in check until he deactivates the bust.

Ritter finds his phone and calls Cindy.

It rings four times before she answers.

"Cin, the Easter Bunny just tried to whack me," Ritter informs her without preamble. "Clear out of your apartment now and muster with the team at Sin du Jour."

"What in *the* pan-fried hell are you—" Cindy begins to say.

Then she yells an unintelligible curse and the line goes dead.

PART II

THE FALSE IDOLS

PROLOGUE, TAKE TWO:
BRONKO IN HELL

The microscopic section of his consciousness that is still sane and rational has kept a running tally of how many times Bronko has butchered his own corpse in front of a live studio audience.

This will mark the seven hundred forty-third consecutive time he's plunged a knife into his butterflied body cavity.

"See, folks, you wanna start at the joint here." Bronko's voice is hoarse and far beyond weary. His hands, one gripping his large-bladed Kauffman and the other gripping his surrogate's hip, are numb.

It never ends. Sometimes he runs, like he did the first time, but he always finds himself back on the set. When he completes the show, turning his own flesh into aromatic party appetizers that are passed among the plastic studio audience to consume like threshing machines, he's led off the set and then right back onto it to shoot the episode all over again.

Bronko's knife hand shakes uncontrollably above the body that is his and yet not his. His other hand digs into that necrotic hip until it leaves bruises.

"You just wanna . . . you just wanna go ahead and . . . you just take your knife, see . . ."

The audience waits patiently, happily, their wide, radiant smiles never wavering.

Don't look at 'em, Bronko tells himself. Just don't look at 'em.

But he does. He raises his head and stares past the ceaselessly rolling cameras at the automatons in their pastel sweaters that might as well be a single, grotesque organism.

Those goddamn plastic smiles with their teeth as white as insane asylum walls just stare right back.

It's that manic sea of fake joy more than anything that finally collapses Bronko, even more than the macabre task of treating an exact copy of his own body as butchering meat for the grill hundreds upon hundreds of times.

His mind finally snaps.

Bronko reverses his grip on the giant kitchen knife, wrapping his other hand around its ergonomic handle and, with a bellowing shriek, plunging the tip of the blade into the center of his forehead.

He manages to drive almost four inches of the knife through his skull before the dense and murky depths of his brain halt its progress. Bronko continues shrieking, hands relinquishing the knife's handle and arms falling to his sides. A curtain of blood falls over his eyes, breaking into a dozen thick streams that trickle down to his jawline. The blood is warm on his face while a cool rush spreads through the rest of his body, and in a bizarre way it's almost comforting.

He continues shaking and yelling for several more seconds until he finally has to accept that his screeching is manufactured. There's no pain, none at all. He's also still utterly conscious and aware. Having four inches of Damascus steel embedded in his brain hasn't stopped or even slowed its function. Bronko blinks away the blood and his eyes go cross as he stares up at the gargantuan kitchen knife sticking out of his forehead.

It might as well be a Halloween costume.

"Cut!" the show's director yells, exasperated, from behind the cameras. "Bronko, I just don't think we're gettin' it today. I'm calling it. We'll try again tomorrow, all right?"

Bronko stares past the searing lights at the man. He's still breathing heavily, mostly from the exertion of screaming his lungs out and jamming the knife in his skull. He's covered in his own blood down to his waist.

Bronko just nods, dumbly.

"Good deal," the director calls back. "That's a wrap, everybody!"

Everything happens very fast then, and with an antlike efficiency. Twentysomething grips wearing black T-shirts branded with the show's logo appear from the shadows, breaking the set down wordlessly. The hooded attendants wheel away Bronko's dressed corpse double on its slab. The island with its gas burners and all of Bronko's ingredients follows it, while the backdrop is whisked away in the opposite direction. The cameras are carried off. Even the grandstand is pulled apart, those hollow shells of an audience still smiling in their seats, and each section is steered off into the shadowy recesses of the studio.

A grip runs up and grasps the handle of the knife still buried in Bronko's skull. The young crewmember yanks it free effortlessly and silently, bringing a towel up with their other hand and wiping down Bronko's face before disappearing.

Lastly, those bright, burning stage lights are all extinguished.

Bronko is left standing alone in the midst of a now empty set in almost total darkness.

It might be minutes or hours later when he hears the squeaking of small wheels.

Those same hooded attendants from before push into view the same red door through which Bronko tried in vain to escape so many times. It's held in a freestanding wooden frame with wheels on the bottom. They halt a few feet in front of them and one of the attendants grips the knob and begins to slowly twist it open.

Bronko braces himself, ready for anything, for the devil himself.

Instead what looks like a five-foot-tall accountant steps

through from the nothing on the other side of the door.

Bronko blinks down at the man. He's wearing a gray suit with a red vest and tie and carrying an old-fashioned gym teacher's clipboard, a pencil sharpened near to the nub held between two of his fingers like a cigarette. He's middle-aged, wears wire-rimmed spectacles, and his receding hairline stinks of cheap styling gel.

"All right, then, Chef Luck," the nebbishy man begins, touching the tip of his stubby golf pencil to the end of his tongue. "Your time here has officially concluded. We'll be moving you on to your final venue of reflection and torment. I'll just need your signature—"

"What place?" Bronko interjects. "What . . . final? What else is there?"

The little man shrugs. "I'm just a clerk, really, I'm sure I don't know. But I will need your signature for processing—"

"Please, just tell me," Bronko pleads, tears welling in both of his eyes.

The clerk sighs, flipping through the pages in his clipboard. "Very well, if it'll get you to stop interrupting a celestial entity just trying to do their job. You're going to—"

The clerk frowns suddenly.

This time it isn't Bronko that's interrupted his train of thought.

"Oh, now wait just a darn minute here . . ."

"What?" Bronko demands, on the verge of mania.

"Well . . . this form should've been on top, not on the bottom. That Freda at intake, this is the fourth time this—"

"What's happening?" Bronko practically screams.

"You're not supposed to be here at all. This is a third-party possession instrument I'm looking at. Your soul has been preempted. Another entity holds the claim on it. This is really darn aggravating for me. I am on a schedule here."

Understanding washes over Bronko in a cool, cleansing wave. He leans his head back and closes his eyes, breathing deeply.

"Boys," he hears the clerk say, "flush him while I sort this file out. The paperwork this is going to take, I swear—"

Hands with iron grips seize his arms and Bronko's attention snaps back to find the hooded attendants forcing him toward the open door with nothing on the other side. He struggles instinctively, but the strength of their hold is inhuman.

"Wait!" Bronko insists. "What's going to happen? Where am I—"

His words turn to unintelligible cries as his body is hurled through the doorway.

He doesn't appear on the other side.

THE PARTY

"Underwhelmed" is the wrong word to describe Lena's experience at her first Hollywood party.

"Bored as monkey fuck" is the phrase that comes more naturally to mind.

There are the celebrities, of course. That had some initial cachet; occupying the same physical space as people she's seen so prominently featured on movie and television screens, in magazines, and who always seem so fascinating on talk shows because the show's host is usually adept at reacting to whatever they say as if it's the most relevant, entertaining, urgent thing they've ever heard.

It takes fifteen minutes for the amusement of that to wear away for Lena.

Then she realizes there's nothing meaningful or particularly interesting about seeing a celebrity in person, or even meeting one briefly.

They're not even particularly attractive to look at, she decides.

They're just . . . more *polished* than people who don't make their living being photographed.

That's what makes them look different.

It's not that they're scads more attractive, they're just all so damn polished and put together and exercised and outfitted by teams of professionals who know how to disguise a regular human being in celebrity camouflage.

They're just grossly overgroomed people.

It's a disappointing thing to know.

Lena spends two hours behind a modest buffet table set near the wall of the lavish penthouse space. She staffs several chafing dishes, scooping tofu poached in coconut milk and lemongrass or ginger-and-lime mushrooms and zucchini into lettuce cups and topping it with Thai chile peanut rémoulade at the guests' requests. There are also ready-to-serve seared ahi tuna medallions, squash fritters, and garlic eggplant skewers.

It's not particularly inspired food, but it's not a crowd of particularly inspiring eaters.

She recognizes several famous faces from the royal goblin wedding they catered, but none of them seem to recognize her.

She doubts any of them are even the slightest bit aware it's the same company catering this event.

Why the hell would they be?

Not even regular-ass, nonfamous people remember who made the food at a party.

Mr. Mirabel, Pacific, and the servers he hired locally

circulate silently and unobtrusively among the guests, ferrying trays of the low-calorie and/or vegan hors d'oeuvres Lena is still ashamed she helped conceive and prepare.

She watches Pacific, lost in his own world walled by the earbuds tucked deftly into his ears, wearing his perpetual friendly smile. His serving hand seems to operate expertly and independently of the rest of him. Not a single guest reaching for one misses the organic smoked paprika cranberry-glazed turkey mini-sliders on quinoa crisps (the damn grain is its own religion out here, it seems, and baked bread is a sacrilege).

She begged Bronko to let them do a fried mozzarella slider as the vegetarian option, but he reminded her, mock-haughtily, that the mandate for this event was "vegan." She realizes now he already had a full menu in mind, but he let them grapple with the problem anyway, probably because it amused him.

Lena tried her hand at a smoked turnip and kale slider, and while the kale turned out pretty good the turnip was like a sponge no matter how she spiced or cooked it.

It consoled her little that Darren's own experiment with leek sliders was worse.

Way worse.

They admitted defeat to Bronko, who then, in fifteen

minutes, whipped up a vegan slider featuring a patty he made from ground black beans and chickpeas.

It was impossibly delicious.

It reminded Lena that their executive chef became famous originally because, past his huge stature and personality, he is a genius at developing deep, amazing flavors in simple foods.

Lena staffs her station and watches the polished throng mill and circulate and chatter at each other, taking selfies to post to their Instagram accounts so they can Tweet and Facebook the Instagram links.

The male lead of the movie they're all celebrating Snapchats in front of her table for five whole minutes.

He tells her the squash fritters are "sick."

Despite the demons and goblins and leprechauns and Hollywood celebrities, working for Sin du Jour has never felt more like an everyday grind to Lena.

She looks over at Darren, staffing the fresh smoothies station. He's done a brisk trade in nut butter smoothies all night, visibly having to stuff giggles every time somebody orders one.

She's still kind of pissed at him, but Lena can't help smiling at that.

"Lemme get one of those eggplant kabob deals," a smooth, masculine voice bids her.

Lena turns back to her task and finds herself face to

face with Producer One, smiling beatifically at her.

Lena retrieves one of the skewers and folds a napkin around it carefully, handing it to the man.

"I produced the film we're celebrating," he informs her without being asked.

"Oh," Lena says, caught off-guard. "We didn't get to see it."

"That's cool. That just means you'll buy a ticket."

He takes a bite of one of the eggplant rounds lanced by the skewer.

The producer makes a satisfied sound as he chews.

"Not bad. So, you work with the infamous Bronko Luck?"

"I work for him, yes."

"Like the gig?"

Lena forces a thin, professional smile and just nods.

The producer laughs. "I can see, yeah. You digging LA, at least?"

"You've got excellent tacos," she says neutrally.

He nods. "Fuck Trump, I say. Let 'em all come over here as long as they're cookin'."

He finishes his skewer, oblivious to how distasteful she obviously finds his humor.

"So," he says, wiping his manicured fingers with the napkin, "is this your first movie premiere?"

Lena nods stiffly.

"Not impressed?"

"It's ... different than I expected," she carefully replies.

He leans over the table and whispers. "Kind of dull, huh?"

Lena half-shrugs.

The producer nods, then a wicked grin forms on his lips.

"Just wait till the after-party, my dear."

He winks and walks away.

Lena's spent the evening elbow-deep in foodstuffs, but it's the first time that night she's longed for a shower.

The party begins winding down surprisingly early. The penthouse crowd thins and what's left of the food goes largely ignored.

Lena's not sure what she expected, but it wasn't this.

Eventually Bronko appears through the increasingly sparse crowd.

A few people even recognize him and stop him to say hello and snap a picture with their phones.

"So?" he asks, approaching her station.

Lena shrugs. "They liked it. I guess. No returns, anyway."

Bronko grins at that, but it's clear he cares even less about this party than she does.

"Well, brace yourself, girl. Jett and Nikki are ready to

light the candle on the after-party. You and Vargas and Pac's crew start breaking down up here, get the leftovers wrapped, and then get downstairs."

Lena stares up at him quizzically.

"What's going to happen downstairs?"

This time Bronko's grin is different.

Lena isn't sure whether to be excited or frightened.

LOS MUERTOS

Cindy returns home after her fourth straight night of eating dinner at Abyssinia, quite possibly the best Ethiopian restaurant outside of Ethiopia itself. She'd never eaten nor had any desire to eat Ethiopian food before moving to New York, and only tried the restaurant initially because she found herself living a few blocks up from its small, nondescript storefront on West 135th Street. Now she's thoroughly addicted, and eats her weight in lentil-filled sambusa on a weekly basis.

Cindy's condo is comfortable, even luxurious. It's unburdened by tchotchkes, or even more personal mementos. She'd wanted, initially, to settle in an older, more historic building, but the steadily shifting demographics in central Harlem (which includes Cindy seeing depressingly fewer black faces than she expected) made the hunt frustrating. In the end she bought in one of the many burgeoning condo developments that dominate the landscape, not only replacing ornate pre-war co-ops with travertine and marble and perfectly square drywall, but erasing the history of the neighborhood and the identity of the people who built and sustained it.

Cindy enters her unit with two large shopping bags and a small plastic one, its handles tied together around the container of leftovers from the restaurant. The latter she stashes quickly in her refrigerator. The other two she carries into the bedroom.

She sets the shopping bags on her bed. From the first she removes a long, carefully wrapped parcel.

She's generally thrifty to a fault, forgoing lavish meals, transportation, entertainment, or even amenities like a private sauna or a big-screen TV.

Cindy does, however, cultivate two expensive vices: antique weapons and designer fashion.

She tears away the parcel's wrapping to reveal a beautiful example of eighteenth-century British naval boarding axes, purchased from an auction house in SoHo that afternoon. Cindy runs her hands over the wood grain, around the simple wedge shape of the axe head.

She's already prepared a spot on the far wall, which is dominated by her collection of fighting axes, tomahawks, and several smaller blades.

Cindy hangs the boarding axe in its chosen spot and stands back to admire her work.

Several moments later she returns to the other shopping bag and withdraws several shoe boxes bearing the Kate Dégradé logo and a single Philipp Plein wrap gown the color of Bordeaux wine, carefully preserved in plastic.

She trains with the weapons often and with great joy in the guest room she's converted into a modest dojo, covering the space where a bed might go with tatami mats.

The clothes, shoes, boots, and other accessories remain untouched and in perfect, alphabetized order throughout several closets, the main one on the other side of her bed.

She's never worn any of it, not a single item, not even on special occasions or to formal events (not that she attends many of those).

She simply never learned how. Raised by a single father and with three brothers there was no one to make such things a priority, let alone teach her. Cindy wasn't even aware of fashion or aesthetics until she was well into her twenties, and despite falling deeply in love with both, she's never developed a context for it in her very practical, utilitarian world. While she adores the fantasy of it, the reality of stepping out into everyday life bereft of her usual uniform doesn't fit her perception of herself.

Still, it remains a quiet passion her job affords her the opportunity to indulge herself in at will. She also follows a wealth of fashion blogs, Twitters, and Tumblrs. She's seen every season of *Project Runway*.

Occasionally Cindy will even hold an outfit in front

of her and look into the mirror, or wear the shoes around her condo while she's relaxing. She loves the feel of an Inbal Dror evening gown against her skin as much as the wood of an ancient battle axe handle in her hand, but in the same way she'd never wield her antique weapons out in the field, she'd never leave her condo in anything other than her surplus BDU pants, tank top, boots, and a sports bra.

The thought of pieces from either of her collections being damaged or ruined is as distasteful to Cindy as what other people might assume about her if they saw her with or in those pieces.

She hears her phone's default ring and realizes she left it in the living room.

Walking briskly from the bedroom and retrieving it, she smiles when she sees Ritter's name on her smart phone's screen.

He's probably drunk. He'll often drunk-dial her to explain some fight scene in whatever movie he's watching and why it works or doesn't.

The boy has a charm despite himself, she always thinks.

Cindy answers the call.

"Cin, the Easter Bunny just tried to whack me," Ritter informs her without preamble. "Clear out of your apartment now and muster with the team at Sin du Jour."

"What in *the* pan-fried hell are you—"

Cindy stops talking and holds the phone away when she sees the first giant flaming pumpkin about to smash through her living room window.

She sees it, even if she can't yet fully reconcile that's what it is.

As the glass shatters she's preparing to dive onto her couch. Every part of her avoids the gargantuan flaming gourd except for her hand. The pumpkin knocks the phone from it, melting the small illuminated screen, and sears the meat of her palm.

She clutches her hand against her abdomen in shock and surprise, watching as a broad, dark figure sails through the window, breaking away what glass is left.

Black, rotted robes flit around a headless body. It hovers there in her living room, levitating several feet off the carpet and away from the window it just destroyed.

Cindy quickly observes it's less a "body" underneath the cloak and capes and more of a skeleton.

One fleshless hand holds aloft a jack-o'-lantern carved with a classic, jagged-tooth visage.

The jack-o'-lantern is alive.

She knows because it begins laughing at her.

The thing's other skeletal hand reaches inside its cloak and pulls out another, uncarved pumpkin.

It quickly and magically comes aflame.

She dives onto her couch, narrowly avoiding the absurd yet deadly projectile.

Cindy bolts from the couch and slips deftly around the corner of the living room into the hallway.

She can hear the horror-movie-villain laughter booming behind her, following.

In her bedroom, Cindy grabs a custom RMJ Shrike tomahawk with one hand and a used Vietnam War–era Peter LaGana tactical tomahawk with the other, ignoring the burning pain in it.

She turns back toward the bedroom door just as the Great Pumpkin or whoever-the-fuck-it's-supposed-to-be hurls another flaming pumpkin at her.

Cindy swings the Shrike, slicing through it cleanly and sending the two halves breaking apart against opposite walls, showering herself with orange muck and seed-dappled tendrils.

In almost the same motion she cocks the hand holding the LaGana tomahawk and launches it at Jack Skeleton. The slender axe flies end over end until the blade sinks into the middle of the thing's chest.

The creature jilts backward a full step, but that's pretty much the totality of the normally fatal blow's impact.

The jack-o'-lantern perpetually perched in its right hand laughs a shrill, terrifying laugh at her.

Its host reaches under its rotted cloaks and produces

another pumpkin, which magically comes aflame.

Cindy instinctively dives below the side of her bed, narrowly avoiding the thing as it goes sailing over her in midair.

Cindy lands on the carpet unharmed.

However, the flaming pumpkin explodes in the recesses of the closet behind her, incinerating thousands upon thousands of dollars in beloved high fashion.

Cindy's head pops up above the bed.

She is lightning moonshine pissed.

"Oh-no-you-motherfucking-did-not-you-goat-shit-veined-sack-of-mule-dung—"

The rest of the rapid-fire curses degenerate into a guttural war cry as she leaps up and jumps onto the bed, using it and her momentum like a trampoline to launch herself directly at the creature that's just destroyed her precious babies.

The thing doesn't have time to ready another pumpkin bomb.

The jack-o'-lantern's laughter turns into a surprised, panicked shriek as Cindy, both hands wrapped around the handle of the tomahawk, brings its blade down into its thick orange hide, obliterating it in the skeletal creature's hand.

The shriek twists into a sound of intense pain and then ceases altogether.

The eviscerated body holding the jack-o'-lantern loses whatever spark animated it to begin with, collapsing to the carpet, lifeless and inert.

The remains of the chopped jack-o'-lantern roll away from its spindly bone perch.

Cindy stomps on it with her booted foot, still cursing and shouting, until she realizes she's only further ruining carpet she'll have to pay to replace.

She stops.

She stands there, shoulders rising and falling with every heavy breath, staring at the carnage. Then she remembers/realizes her closet is on fire. Cindy dashes to the kitchen and retrieves the fire extinguisher she keeps under the sink. It takes her a full minute to eradicate all the flames.

Everything in the closet is ruined and the walls surrounding it are burnt black. She wishes with everything she is that she could kill that fucking thing again, several times, but for now there's nothing to be done.

Twenty minutes later Cindy is sitting on the lid of the toilet in her master bathroom, securing a medical Velcro patch on the bandage wound tightly and expertly around her burnt hand. A first-aid kit is open beside her on the sink.

The sound of her front door being kicked open is followed immediately by Ritter's voice calling her name, which is the only reason Cindy sighs instead of bolts to her feet.

"I'm in here!" she yells.

Ritter is in her bathroom in three seconds flat.

"Did you kick in my door?" she asks him irritably, ignoring the slightly startled look on his face.

"Uh. Yeah."

"Did knocking not occur to you at any point?"

"Sorry."

Cindy shakes her head. "It's all right. Don't mean to give you shit. What's happening?"

"It's a hit," Ritter says. "We're all being targeted. No one's answering phones. We have to go. Now."

Cindy nods, steeling herself and rising to her feet.

"Who's targeting us?" she asks.

Ritter is already out the door of the bathroom when he calls back to her, nonplussed: "Hell."

ROANOKE

Hara owns a formerly abandoned factory in one of the worst neighborhoods in the South Bronx. He occupies the second floor as his living space, and if Ritter and Cindy's lavish homes can be called "Spartan," the appropriate word to describe Hara's home is "barren." He sleeps on several bare mattresses all pushed together on the immaculately clean floor. The only furniture is a milk crate filled with paperback books new and old and covering a variety of esoteric subjects.

One of the few non-work-related sentences he's ever spoken to Ritter was to express his dislike of owning anything that can't be carried on a horse.

The first floor of the converted factory is what shines. Hara has turned it into something like an eclectic children's museum. Most of it is dominated by a dojo in which he teaches local and other borough kids a variety of martial arts ranging from kyokushin karate to kurash (a Turkic form of wrestling in which competitors grapple with each other by sashes worn around the waist; always a good bloodless way to squash the inevitable beefs that arise between children).

Most of the kids, of course, come to learn how to fight.

Many end up staying to learn what else Hara has to teach.

He has stations erected throughout the back of the space, all of which he built himself. There's a puppet theater where he stages small historical plays (no one knows, but Hara carves all of the delicate, shockingly accurate puppets himself, as well). There are language and technology labs. There are metal and woodworking shops where the kids can build anything they can imagine. There's a reading room and a sewing room (the boys are always tentative, even crude about it until Hara hunkers over one of the vintage machines and begins stitching his own clothing).

All are welcome, free of charge and at any hour, as long as they respect Hara's one very simple rule: Treat all property and people the way you wish to be treated.

Everyone gets a second chance when they break that rule the first time.

A third chance is rarely required.

Likewise, Hara has only had one incident of vandalism and theft. The police never found the perpetrators. The reason they never found them quickly circulated throughout the neighborhood and beyond.

No one has violated the sanctity of the space since.

Hara naturally gets a lot of questions about himself. He answers few of them. No one is even sure what ethnicity he is or isn't, and that may be a reason he's so readily accepted by all.

Ritter and Cindy arrive at the factory to find a gaping hole ripped in the heavy metal hanging door that serves as the main entrance. What appear to be golf ball–sized bullet holes pockmark the area around it. The smell of burnt metal lingers on the air, and some of the depressions are still smoking.

Still, there's nothing but silence beyond.

They quickly run inside through the largest hole in the door.

The two find Hara as they usually find him here, standing stoically by himself on the large sparring mat in the center of the space, lost in whatever complex multitasking his mind occupies itself with while the rest of his mountainous form conserves energy.

There are a couple of key differences, however.

Hara is slathered in what would look like blood, except it's dark green, more like sludge in texture, and stinks inhumanly.

The other unusual element is the pile of mostly decapitated, far-rotting corpses at his feet all dressed like pilgrims from a period film about early American colonization, complete with giant belt buckles and stovepipe hats (which many of the lopped-off, rotted heads are still wearing).

There are muskets with their muzzles flared like Victrola horns scattered about the mat.

Like the holes in the main door, some of them are still smoking.

Hara's breathing is only slightly elevated, and he's still holding the head of one of the rotted corpses by its greasy hair in one hand.

"Zombie pilgrims?" Cindy asks, surveying the carnage. "For real, though?"

"Better than a giant goddamn turkey, I guess," Ritter remarks.

Cindy shakes her head. "No more big-ass birds. Not ever."

"Is this all of them?" Ritter asks Hara.

The giant nods.

"All right. Hose yourself down and meet us at Sin du Jour. We're going for Moon. There's a lot more going on."

Hara nods again.

Ritter turns and heads back out the door, Cindy at his flank.

"What's going after Moon?" she asks him. "Santa Claus?"

Ritter's voice is heavy and grim when he replies, "I

hope not."

"You're serious right now?"

Ritter throws her a look that says he's deathly serious.

Cindy sighs. "Okay, then. I guess we gotta go save his skinny white shanks. But after that I want to know what the fuck is going on."

She pauses, and it's clear it was more of a question than it sounded.

"Yeah, I guess we gotta save him," she repeats, with more finality.

Ritter grins to himself.

EROS

It's difficult to tell whether Moon's apartment has been ransacked or whether this is how it's supposed to look.

While the rest of the team took time and care and put thought into where they settled upon relocating to New York City with their fat signing bonuses and copious new, hazard pay–filled salaries, Moon simply picked the first shithole he found on Craigslist that's relatively close to the office. It's a first-floor walk-up in Jamaica, Queens. Ritter and Cindy make the trek up the broken brick steps to find the lock on the door busted.

Cindy unsheathes a large dagger from beneath her coat and frees her tactical tomahawk from its tie-down rig on her leg, holding both weapons at the ready.

She nods at Ritter.

He opens the door and they move strategically inside, covering the conceivable blind spots beyond and each other.

The front room seems empty at first.

Well, "empty" may be a misnomer.

Moon gets most of his meals in a box from Crown

Fried Chicken around the corner from his building, and most of those boxes are scattered on the floor, or filling every useable inch of space atop the Ikea furniture.

The coffee table is the only sacred space, and that is because it's piled high and corner to corner with weed paraphernalia.

Stale fried chicken and bong water is a less than welcoming olfactory combination.

The one slightly kept spot in the whole space is Moon's entertainment center.

They always wondered what he did with his money.

Towering shelves of every video gaming console and equipment imaginable wall a dominating 110-inch television, the largest either of them has ever seen in a home. Most of the game consoles are new if not outright futuristic-looking, but a few vintage systems are included. Many are covered in non-English writing. The shelves end in speakers that are less like speakers and more like columns in a Greek ruin.

"My God. I knew this day would come," Cindy remarks, mock-darkly. "And it's even worse than I imagined."

"Focus," Ritter says.

"On what?"

Then they hear the gentle weeping.

It's coming from the corner.

They peer through the *Hoarders* episode of Moon's front room and see a slight figure curled up there.

The figure is completely hidden under a blanket, but visibly shivering and convulsing with each new spasm of tears.

"Moon?" Ritter ventures carefully, weaving toward the corner. "It's okay, pal. Whatever happened, it's okay."

He reaches out and grips the rough-hewn blanket, easing it away gently.

"Aw, what the fuck is that now?" Cindy asks, Ritter's brows furrow in confusion.

"It's Cupid," he pronounces, no hesitation, no doubt.

The three-foot-tall creature curled up in the corner of Moon's apartment certainly fits that bill. The bloated cheeks of its cherub's face are more swollen than any human's could possibly be. It has small, harplike wings, and is indeed clutching a crude-looking bow, a quiver of arrows strapped to its back.

It pays no attention to Ritter, or even acknowledges their presence.

It seems totally absorbed in its own miserable state, continuing to weep unabated.

"Damn thing shot me in the ass!" Moon shouts at them from behind.

Ritter and Cindy both spin around in surprise, Cindy raising knife and tomahawk at the ready.

Moon stands in the entrance to his kitchen, fisting a bag of Cool Ranch Doritos.

He's bare from the waist down except for a pair of tighty whities that appear to be a size small even for him.

"Dammit, Moon," Ritter chastises.

"Boy, put some pants on!" Cindy demands, shielding her eyes with one arm.

"I can't," Moon complains, turning three-quarters to reveal a bloody bandage hastily and sloppily applied to his right butt cheek.

"Then wrap a towel around your waist! Damn!"

He shrugs, popping another chip into his mouth. "No clean ones."

"I'mma faint from surprise."

"It shot you?" Ritter asks, talking over their bickering as he's often forced to do. "With an arrow."

Moon nods. "I think it was supposed to make me sad or something. I dunno. The spell must have bounced back onto him. He's been crying like a little bitch for over an hour. I can't get him to leave!"

Ritter and Cindy exchange baffled looks. They've both seen his body's natural ability to repel curses, hexes, and other harmful spells in the magical food he ingests (his one and only practical value to the team), but this is another level.

Cindy openly marvels at him. "I don't know what you

could have possibly done so right in a past life."

Moon doesn't even hear her. "And look at this shit here!"

Moon limps past them, over to his video gaming shrine.

He picks up what looks like a futuristic headset that's been mostly smashed.

"He fucking broke my PlayStation VR, man!" Moon whines. "This was a prototype. Fuckin' *burns* that Oculus Rift vaporware bullshit. Now it's chucked. Do you know how hard it was to get? No, fuck that. *Impossible* to get?"

"You're lucky to be alive, you asshole," Cindy says. "This thing came here to kill you."

Moon stares at her suddenly, mouth agape, then he looks over at the shrilly weeping Cupid.

"Oh."

Cindy nods. "Yeah."

Moon looks back at them, wearing a confused expression.

"Why? What'd I do now?"

"I'll explain on the way," Ritter says. "For now, find some pants and let's go. You can sit on one ass cheek if you need to. We've got to get to Sin du Jour."

Moon gestures to Cupid with his rumpled Doritos bag. "What about him?"

Ritter looks around briefly.

"What damage is he going to do, Moon?"

Moon recognizes that as a slam on his place, but he can't seem to work up the indignance to retort.

"Yeah, fine. Whatever."

He limps off to the small bedroom in the back, presumably to find pants.

"Did I tell you Pumpkin Dick torched my collection?" Cindy asks Ritter.

"Arms or dresses?"

"All my fashion."

"Oh," Ritter says, suddenly and noticeably less interested. "Sorry."

Cindy frowns. "I need more friends with lady parts."

"We work with a bunch of 'em."

Cindy just grunts.

"Hey!" Moon calls to them from the back. "Can one of you check my ass bandage?"

Cindy's eyes widen.

"That is *all* you," she informs Ritter.

HORSE SHIT

After hours in Sin du Jour's main kitchen, Dorsky fills six shot glasses with Wild Turkey for him and his line.

Rollo, Chevet, and Tenryu all gather around the station where Dorsky is serving.

James, having spent the evening bailing sea-salt-and-vinegar-speckled hay onto minotaurs' plates the size of manhole covers, finishes wiping down a pair of newly cleansed and sterilized pitchforks, and hangs them both on a rack filled with likewise unusual implements for a fine-dining kitchen.

"James, let's do this thing!" Dorsky barks at him in his usual gruff line boss way.

"You got it, Chef," James says, unperturbed, and jogs quickly over to the station where the shots are waiting.

"I poured an extra one for you there, My Horse Has the Trots-skys," Dorsky tells Rollo.

The rotund, bearded Russian is the only one of them who has already showered and changed out of his serving whites.

Chevet, Tenryu, and James laugh, not because it's a

particularly good pun (it's not), but because the memory of a drunken centaur lifting his tail and expelling the remains of the dinner Rollo so diligently helped prepare all over him will never not be funny to them.

"Goddamn half-and-half abominations, all of them," Rollo grumbles in his thick accent, downing the first shot immediately and picking up the other one to toast.

Dorsky, suppressing his own laughter, raises a shot to them.

"To a job well done, and to not having to serve a wine-soaked barnyard for another year," he toasts.

They all touch shot glasses and throw back their contents.

James coughs several times after, unaccustomed to hard liquor on anything resembling a regular basis.

Rollo holds his empty shot glass up to the light, examining it ruefully. "What you think newbies are doing right now? Eh? Rubbing asses with movie stars who do not accidentally shit on you?"

Dorsky shrugs. "Bronko wants 'em under his wing until they're ready to fly on they're own, that's all. He did the same thing with your big, dumb Cossack ass. He did it with all of us. It's his way."

Rollo grunts, but he can't argue with the truth of that statement, any of it.

"Y'all did good tonight," Dorsky tells them, sounding

very much like Bronko in that moment. "Any asshole can fork hay and cut up apples, it takes a real goddamn chef to cook the hell out of it so it's real people food. And that's what we do. Turn bullshit into real damn food."

"You mean horse shit, oui?" Chevet asks.

That sets them all off laughing again.

Except for Rollo, naturally.

He pours himself another shot and downs it.

Dorsky looks up, his laughter fading as he stares across the kitchen at Boosha, occupying the entrance arch with a severe look on her ancient, slightly inhuman face.

He's never seen Sin du Jour's resident ancient foods and culture expert outside of her ramshackle apothecary, let alone in his kitchen.

"What's up, Boosh?" he asks neutrally.

"Something comes," she says with a heavy, if vague, finality.

Rollo looks to Dorsky with a derisive laugh and questioning eyes. "What she says?"

Dorsky just shakes his head, his attention on Boosha.

The inside of his stomach suddenly feels hollow, and the booze he just put there stings.

"What's coming?" he asks the old woman.

"I smelt eyes of oracle in pot. Read signs. I have little oracle in me. Something comes for us tonight. Something unnatural. Something . . . from below."

"Bullshit," Rollo immediately insists.

"Horse shit?" Tenryu offers.

He, Chevet, and James share another chuckle.

Dorsky frowns, familiar with Boosha's occasional inability to retrieve not only English, but human words.

"'Below'?" he asks her.

Before Boosha can explain further, the room and the entire building around it is rocked from side to side with a deafening boom, hard enough to smash an overhead light and rain plaster dust from the ceiling and walls.

They all grasp the station counter to steady themselves.

Boosha braces her brittle-looking form against the frame of the archway.

All of their ears are ringing.

It sounds like a bomb has gone off somewhere in the front of the building.

James runs over to the archway where Boosha stands, both of them looking around the corner of the main kitchen.

However, the lights suddenly cut out before they have the chance to peer down the corridor to where it opens onto Sin du Jour's lobby.

But they all hear the screams that erupt from that direction.

Dorsky stands and walks over to a magnetic strip of two-foot-long butchering knives bolted to the far wall.

He grips the handle of one of them and rips its blade free of the strip.

"Everybody out of the kitchen!" he instructs his line and Boosha. "Head for the back and go out the service entrance. James, you're in charge of the old lady."

"Am not old lady!" Boosha fires back, incensed.

"Do it now!" Dorsky thunders, his voice more powerful and commanding than any of them have ever heard it.

At the entrance, James takes Boosha gently by the arm.

Chevet and Tenryu move to join them.

Rollo walks over to his regular station and reaches to the hanging rack above it, pulling down a meat cleaver blade affixed to a two-handed haft.

He looks to Dorsky. "I am with you," he says, and it's not a question.

Dorsky just nods.

Together the two of them usher the others through the archway, and, blades held aloft, they plunge into the darkness beyond.

SATURNALIA

Ritter's Acura TL and Hara's Gunbus turn onto 10th Street from opposite directions at almost the same time.

Ritter signals to the giant on the absurdly large motorcycle, and Hara falls into formation behind him.

They drive up the street toward the corner where the dusty red brick fortress that is Sin du Jour sits.

Ritter is forced to stop short suddenly several yards away because of a large object blocking the middle of the street. They all quickly realize it's Sin du Jour's front doors, and each one has been folded in half.

Apprehension bubbles in Ritter's throat like acid and he chokes it back.

"Jesus," Cindy whispers beside him in the front seat.

"What is it?" Moon asks from the back seat.

Without answering, Ritter kills the engine and hits his hazard lights, disembarking quickly from the car.

The others follow suit.

Running around the vehicle, Ritter pops the trunk and removes a bulky surplus duffel bag, slinging it over his shoulder.

"What's that?" Cindy asks.

"Backup," is all Ritter says as he sprints to the exposed front entrance of the building into the dark interior.

Ritter's orders come fast and resolute. "Hara, go around back to the service entrance, see if you can find Ryland. Meet us in the middle. Moon, go with him."

"I need to get a gun or something," Moon whines, but doesn't protest further.

He follows Hara down the sidewalk and around the corner.

Beside Ritter, Cindy unsheathes her weapons.

They enter Sin du Jour slowly and with extreme vigilance.

"Why didn't the security system kick in?" Cindy whispers to him. "The fucked-up cartoon dog thing?"

"Same reason the dampening field in my place didn't work on that fucking demon rabbit," Ritter says. "This isn't Earthly magic. This is the power of Hell itself. It's different. It comes from a different place, a different reality. It can't be contained by earthbound magicks."

"And the things that came after us?"

"The False Idols. It's like Hell's elite hit squad. They're only sent after very select targets. I heard about it years back. I thought it was a myth. Not even that. A bad joke."

"Why would the damn devil create killer Easter Bunnies and fucked-up pumpkin monsters?"

"Because he thinks it's funny? I don't know."

The lobby of Sin du Jour has been completely destroyed. The bunkerlike front desk has been reduced to rubble. Ritter surveys the disaster zone in complete disbelief, his eyes coming to rest on a prone body half-covered in debris.

"Shit!" Ritter sprints forward and slides on his knees beside the body, seeing white hair gleaming even in the darkness.

It's White Horse.

He's still breathing, staccato and pained. There's a large, jagged shard of wood sticking out of his side, blood pooling around it, soaking his faded shirt.

"Can you hear me, Granddad?" Ritter asks.

"Not your damn granddad," White Horse says around wheezing breaths.

Ritter examines the wound as best he can in the dark. "What happened? What's hit us?"

"Ritter!" Cindy calls.

Ritter looks over in alarm, but all he finds is Cindy standing over Little Dove. The girl is hugging her knees against the wall, rocking back and forth, makeup-muddied tears streaking her face.

"Is she hurt?" Ritter asks.

"Shell-shocked, I think."

"She saved me," White Horse says.

"I didn't!" Little Dove suddenly screams. "I didn't do anything! It wasn't me!"

She sounds as if she's trying to convince herself more than them.

Cindy kneels down and puts her arms around the girl.

Rather than fighting it, Little Dove leans into her, sobbing anew.

"She has power," White Horse whispers for Ritter's ears alone. "I had no . . . I didn't know. She has . . . it's too much for her . . . too young . . ."

"All right, all right," Ritter soothes him. "We'll deal with that later. What's here, White Horse? Where are the others?"

The old man just shakes his head.

Ritter sighs. "Okay, fine. Look, don't yank this thing out of your guts. Just leave it. Don't move. You'll be okay. We'll come back for you."

"White lies," the Hataałii says, laughing, and the laughter doesn't seem to cause him half as much pain as the coughing it turns into.

Ritter steadies him with both hands. "Don't start with that shit, all right? I never signed a treaty in my life."

He stands up, walking over to Cindy and Little Dove and crouching down in front of the girl.

He looks up at Cindy. "We need to keep moving, re-con the building, and find the others."

Cindy doesn't speak, but she looks down at Little Dove pointedly.

The girl has stopped sobbing, but she's still clinging to Cindy.

"Lill?" Ritter says softly. "Lill? Look at me, okay?"

Her frightened eyes find his.

Ritter reaches out and pinches the flesh of her arm.

Hard.

"Owwwwwww!" she wails. "What the hell, man?"

Cindy shoves an arm between him and the girl.

"Ritt! Damn!"

"There y'are," he says to Little Dove. "Hi. Look, I don't know what happened to you, and if it sucked I'm sorry, but we don't have time for it right now. Snap out of it and go over to your grandfather. Keep him still and keep him awake. Okay?"

Little Dove stares up at him angrily, rubbing the reddened patch of skin on her arm.

She looks to Cindy, who can only shrug.

"Fine," she says hoarsely. "Yeah. Okay. I've got it."

Ritter nods. "Thank you."

She pries herself away from Cindy and crawls across the floor to where her White Horse is lying.

Cindy stands up, looking at Ritter with obvious displeasure.

"You're a shitty trauma counselor," she says.

"I'll send her a card," he says, his mind already moving on. "Come on."

He strikes off down the hall.

Cindy follows, still frowning.

None of the lights are working in the corridor, either.

It's totally silent.

The space just *feels* abandoned.

Ritter's gut sinks with every step.

They come across the first one several yards before the entrance to the main kitchen. It's a small body lying on its back, even smaller than Cupid. Its face is all sharp, elongated angles like a horrific wooden puppet. It is alive, however, or was, and it has a mouth full of razor-sharp teeth. It's clad in a green tunic, a breadcrumb hat, and pointed shoes.

The shoes and hat both have bells on them.

There's a high-end paring knife sticking out of its right eye.

"That's not—"

"An elf," Ritter confirms. "It's a helper elf."

Cindy stares down at the little monster's corpse darkly.

"So, that means . . ."

PAPERWEIGHTS

"San Nioclás!" Ryland informs them irately. "Daidí na Nollag. Father Christmas. Whatever you want to call the fat bastard, it's him!"

Hara and Moon found Sin du Jour's resident alchemist not far from his perpetually parked RV home, on his hands and knees throwing up liquid the color of blood, but which smelled like sour grapes.

Half a dozen stone statues of demonic Christmas elves in various menacing poses surrounded him.

Now he's sitting on the steps of his booted RV, chain-smoking a cigarette every thirty seconds with vomited wine drying on the same powder-blue dress shirt he always wears.

"Where did all the lawn gnomes come from?" Moon asks, staring at the grotesque miniature statues.

"The North Pole. Obviously."

"Oh, they're elves?"

"They're hellions bereft of any semblance of manners or etiquette!" Ryland all but shrieks, nearly falling from the steps of the RV.

Hara reaches out a hand and encompasses Ryland's entire right shoulder, steadying him.

The drunken alchemist tries to shake him off, but it's a futile attempt.

"So, wait. These things . . . like, they were real? And you turned them into stone?"

"I had little choice in the matter," Ryland says defensively.

"So . . . okay, run it back for us, bro. What all happened?"

Ryland sighs animatedly, dropping the stub of his fifth cigarette on the pavement and lighting a sixth.

"I was enjoying a late supper of gourmet fermented grapes and decidedly nongourmet fermented grapes when I heard a terrible commotion inside. Disturbed, and frankly pained in the head, I sought to investigate. As soon as I opened the door I was set upon by these—"

He waves both arms wildly at the stone elves.

"It was an ambush, I tell you!"

Moon is genuinely impressed.

"How'd you turn them all to stone like that?"

"I don't recall. Quite impressively and expertly, I imagine."

"Okay, wicked, but where does Santa Claus fit into—"

"I saw him! I glimpsed his bright red posterior inside

wreaking havoc on the interior! A great, corpulent fellow. Clearly an anglophile's representation of the beloved seasonal icon. I blame America, frankly."

He's poised to say more, but Ryland's tirade is interrupted by a sudden cacophony from high above them.

They all look up as a large fiery object flies over the side of Sin du Jour's roof three stories above and plunges down to the concrete in front of them.

It hits the pavement with a wet, sickening thud.

"Holy shit!"

"What now?" Ryland whines, leaning back into his RV.

Hara approaches it, examining what appears to be the charred corpse of an animal, one with horns sharpened into scythes and patchy, burnt fur decorated with bones and small skulls.

It's a reindeer, or was.

Hara looks back at Moon and points up, his expression harder than usual.

Moon nods. "Right. Yeah. The roof. Okay." He looks back at Ryland. "Let's go."

"I don't wish to go," Ryland protests. "I'm unwell. I've had a terrible fright and require tea and a brief nap, and also—"

Hara has grabbed him by the shirt before he can finish, hauling him off the RV steps and dragging him along as the three walk to the service entrance.

"Unhand me, you great brute!" Ryland screeches as he's pulled inside the building. "At least allow me to bring my smoking materials, ya bastard!"

THE AFTER-PARTY

It's almost two hours later when Lena and the others have the penthouse party wrapped. They've returned the serving and prep equipment to the hotel's kitchen, vacuum-sealed all the perishable leftovers, and returned everything they brought to their rented vans in the sub-terranean parking structure.

They cut the temp servers loose for the night and she, Darren, Pacific, and Mr. Mirabel make their way to the ground floor of the hotel. VIP signs direct them to a long, empty corridor with high vaulted ceilings like something from an ancient church.

The heavy security at the far end lets them pass.

The other end is marked by a towering set of closed double doors.

More security guards it.

They also grant the foursome entrance based on the cartoon chocolate cake Sin du Jour logos embroidered on the breasts of their smocks.

But first one of the severe-looking two-piece guards asks them, "Y'all have cell phones?"

Lena just stares at him in surprise and confusion at first.

"No," Darren answers for her. "They haven't worked all day."

"Recording devices of any kind?" the guard presses them.

The four of them exchange looks.

"Uh, no, nothing," Lena assures him.

One of the double doors is opened just enough to allow them each to pass through individually.

They're immediately blasted with a sonic lashing of bass-heavy techno music from within.

Lena enters first, followed by the rest. The space is massive, with Italian marble floors and a ceiling forty feet high and dominated by an artisanal stained-glass skylight. Jett has bathed it in constantly shifting lights of deep reds and violets.

But it's not the lighting design or the music that has stricken the two line cooks and two servers dumb with awe.

What they're witnessing is a carnival of culinary sin in full swing and beyond anything Lena could've imagined.

Jett and Nikki have both outdone themselves in their separate areas of expertise.

Not only that, they've married them together to create something of which Lena wouldn't have thought them capable, especially Nikki, who she's come to know as the reserved, cheerful baker making cupcakes in her little kitchen at Sin du Jour.

There's a kaleidoscopic tug-of-war for Lena's attention. Her eyes fall briefly on what look like oversized rubber children's pools filled with melted chocolate. Svelte, gorgeous twentysomething men and women clad in Speedo bikinis are frolicking and play-wrestling in it. Stations are set up around the paddling pools, piled high with skewers of dusted marshmallows, fresh strawberries, and other delicacies guests are picking up and brushing on the chocolate-covered models.

Lena's attention immediately shifts to another station, an arrangement of ornate gurneys upon which more of the beautiful twentysomethings are laid out, covered in succulent pieces of sashimi and sushi rolls.

There's a giant freestanding lobster tank, but the lobsters at the bottom are only two- to three-pound tails that have already been cooked. Instead of water the tank is filled with melted butter being kept at temperature by motorized heaters. At the top of the tank there are literally divers in full-body wet suits emblazoned with the studio logo waiting to dive in the tank and retrieve the meaty, butter saturated tails upon request.

There's an entire installation designed to look like an old, rustic mine cart sitting on a short length of track.

A mound of multicolored gems is piled high inside it. A large spiral drill is erected over the top of the cart. It constantly bathes the gems in an iridescent sauce made of jade that can only be a creation of Ryland's. Famous goblin actors and singers pick at the jewel mountain and pop them in their mouths, crunching up the stones easily and swallowing them.

An entire three-hundred-pound whole hog bathed in a barbeque chocolate sauce is roasting over a mobile fire pit. There are ribbon dancers in elaborate costumes whose ribbons seem to be made of edible licorice.

It's too much for the human mind to process.

"This is fucking insane!" Lena yells over the blaring music.

Darren's smile is half a foot wide across his face with the openness of a child. "This is awesome!"

Behind them, Pacific lights one of his ready-made, expertly rolled joints, takes a puff and passes it to Mr. Mirabel.

"At least we're finally on a gig where we can burn one without getting hassled," Pacific says dreamily.

The very center of the space is quartered off with classic Hollywood theater red velvet ropes and gold-plated posts.

They're protecting what looks to Lena like the world's largest chafing dish, the kind of novelty item roadtrippers cruising through the South would pull over to admire.

The dish is filled with a gleaming red cherries jubilee, the dessert traditionally paired with ice cream and served flambéed.

Except this one is the size of a Scottish hilltop.

It's only awaiting cream and fire.

That must be the evening's grand finale Jett mentioned.

Very few guests from the premiere party upstairs have been allowed access to the after-party, and most of the people here didn't even bother to attend the penthouse affair at all.

This is the VIP crowd.

Most of them Lena doesn't know on sight. The new faces Lena spots that she recognizes don't belong to celebrities, they belong to bona fide legends.

She even thinks she sees a Beatle.

"Yo!"

It's Bronko.

He makes his way to them through the sea of jubilant bodies.

"All good?" he asks Lena.

"Yes, Chef."

"All right, then. Y'all are off the clock."

"Should we go back to the hotel?" Darren asks.

Bronko. "Hell, no! Mix it up a little. Have a good time.

These folks won't notice the difference, not at this point."

He claps Darren on the shoulder and throws Lena a wink before turning and leaving them on their own.

But before he does he snatches the joint from Pacific's lips.

"Party foul!" Pac complains.

Lena eventually finds Nikki staffing a station where guests recline in a massage chair while she creates miniature gourmet ice cream sundaes in their open mouths.

"Hey!" Lena shouts out of necessity, tapping her on the shoulder.

Nikki looks back, sees her, and smiles.

"Oh, hey!"

"How could you not tell me about any of this?" Lena asks, head still spinning.

"I wanted it to be a surprise!" Nikki yells as she drizzles pistachio syrup into the waiting mouth of the star of that big male stripper movie franchise.

"It is," Lena says at a normal volume and in deadpan fashion.

"How'd you do all this?" she asks.

Nikki is now spooning maple walnut ice cream past the lips of the main villain from those blockbuster superhero team movies, who, while not being the traditional definition of movie star sex appeal, she'd personally straddle in that chair and allow to eat the ice cream off of her.

"Uh . . ." She fumbles to respond to Lena, distracted. "Jett's zomb—. . . workers. They helped."

Jett's politically correct views of the undead preclude anyone she works with from referring to her crew as "zombies," even though that's exactly what they fucking are.

"You let them do food prep?" Lena demands, shocked.

Nikki waves away her concerns with her free hand. "We put them in hazmat suits. It's fine. How else were we supposed to get this all set up in three days?"

Three hours go by in a blinding haze.

At one point Lena watches as the stripper movie guy has to be carried out of the after-party.

He's not drunk.

In fact, he didn't have a drop to drink.

He simply ate until he became violently ill and could no longer stand or form cogent sentences.

UP TO THE HOUSETOP THE
COURSERS THEY FLEW

It's a war of blood and fire between Santa Claus, his reindeer and elves, and half a dozen Manhattan-trained chefs on a rooftop in Long Island City.

Only in New York.

Ritter and Cindy burst through the access door to the rooftop, coming upon the scene in full throes.

Dorsky and the line cooks have formed a haphazard skirmish line behind a makeshift barricade of upturned buffet tables on wheels and piles of stainless-steel chafing dishes. They're all armed with the largest kitchen cutlery they could grab; Rollo, the great bear of a man ever by Dorsky's side, is holding the haft of a giant meat cleaver that looks like it came out of the Middle Ages. They've also got chafing dishes full of smaller knives that they're hurling like artillery over the barricade.

Santa Claus is an eight-foot-tall mass of flesh that's more like rawhide and hair that's more like steel wool armor. His beard is as long as an average-sized person all by itself and wide enough to consume several of those. It's decorated with dozens of disturbingly small skulls and likewise bones. He holds a bullwhip as thick as anchor chain in one claw-gauntleted hand, swinging his signature toy sack in the other, though this sack is spiked like the bulbous head of a mace and shoots fireballs out of its bottom.

The Santa from Hell (literally) stands behind the pulpitlike rise of a bone-armored sled. A mammoth's skull with one side caved in adorns the mast. Santa cracks his whip and slings orbs of flame at the chefs' skirmish line, blazing up the cloths still half-covering several of the tables and denting their surfaces.

All the while jolly laughter's psychotic, cocaine-addicted cousin pours from a dark and murky hollow in the top of that macabre beard.

"Ritter!" Dorsky yells as he spots them emerging from the doors. "Hit the deck!"

Ritter wants to yell back at the asshole that he just exposed their position to the enemy, but that would be counterproductive.

Also, he doesn't have time, as that enemy is now charging them.

Several elves armed with tiny yet wickedly curved blades scurry toward Ritter and Cindy.

One of the colossal, monstrous reindeer trudges behind the creatures.

Cindy unleashes a one-armed golf swing with her tomahawk that takes most of the head off the first elf to come at her. She brings that same arm back down on the next elf, chopping him in half like a block of firewood.

Meanwhile, the reindeer picks up speed and lowers its horns, aiming for them both.

Ritter drops the heavy duffel bag slung over his shoulder and reaches inside his coat with deadly purpose.

He pulls out a baseball.

Cindy glances from the charging reindeer to Ritter, looking at him as if he's lost his mind.

Ritter winds up like Nolan Ryan and sends one straight down the pike at a good seventy-five miles an hour.

Three feet in front of the barreling creature the baseball splits open all on its own, its stringy guts falling out.

Instead of hitting the rooftop in a bundled mass, those guts magically uncoil and expand.

They become a net.

The reindeer hits it full force, the impossibly expansive web of string constricted around it and bundling the animal, taking its legs away and sending it sprawling in a heap on its side.

Its momentum sends that heap sliding across the rooftop.

Ritter and Cindy have to dive from its path in opposite directions to avoid being steamrolled.

The bound reindeer crashes against the wall beside
the access door.

Ritter ends up rolling onto his stomach. He's feeling
pretty satisfied with himself until he looks up and sees
another one of the reindeer staring down its steaming,
dripping nose at him.

The reindeer bares impossibly sharp teeth at him in a
ferocious snarl. "Shit," is all Ritter can come up with.

Fortunately Cindy is more eloquent.

She lets her tomahawk do the talking, burying its
blade in the reindeer's neck.

It lets out a thunderous bellow and swings its massive
head at her. Cindy leans in, mostly avoiding the sharp
prongs of its horns, but its cranium is enough to knock
her off her feet.

It gives Ritter time to roll out from under the animal's
mercy and rebound to his feet, but not enough to get
clear of it before the reindeer turns its agonized, infuri-
ated attention back to him.

Ritter thinks about the small hideaway magicks he
has left on his person, wondering if they'll be enough to
subdue a pissed-off Santa's reindeer from Hell.

He's reaching for the first one when Hara appears in
his line of sight, unheard and unseen a second before

that, ever the silent mountain.

Hara wraps his arms around the reindeer's body, almost able to clasp his hands together, and lifts the entire impossibly large animal off its hooves.

It's amazing, even for Hara.

The giant slams the reindeer to the rooftop floor and crushes his weight atop it, grappling it into submission.

"We got this, Ritt!" Moon announces from far, far in the background.

"Yes, what the lad here said," Ryland echoes.

Ritter spares a glance at Cindy.

She's down, but moving, and she doesn't seem to have any major injuries.

Ritter looks back at Moon. "The bag! Toss me the bag!"

Moon looks around, spotting the duffel bag where Ritter dropped it.

He picks it up in both arms and with great effort tosses it to Ritter, who stops its momentum as gently as he can while still catching it.

"Make like a ramp," Ritter yells at Hara as he continues wrestling with the reindeer, trusting his longtime friend to hear and understand.

Ritter backpedals several steps and then breaks into a fast run, charging toward Hara, unzipping the duffel bag.

The giant leans over the reindeer and straightens his

broader-than-broad back.

Ritter bounds up onto him, needing a full step to traverse Hara's spine, then, bracing himself, leaps as fast and high and far as he can off Hara's shoulder.

He's ten feet in the air and twice that distance from Santa's war sled when he swings the open duffel bag, launching its contents at Santa Claus himself.

Dozens upon dozens of brightly colored Easter eggs fly above the rooftop.

Demon Santa has just finished cracking his whip at the chefs' skirmish line for the hundredth time when he catches the arc of the eggs in the corner of one eye. He swivels his massive, bearded head.

His horrific, jolly laughter ceases.

The eggs break upon his face and torso in one epic volley. His screams are the furthest thing from "jolly" imaginable. A hundred awful, lethal things happen to Santa Claus all at once. It's a living tableau of indescribable horror.

In fact, in Hell it will become known as the single most horrific death ever to occur on Earth. That's like winning the Oscar for best picture down there.

In the end he somehow seems to melt, invert, expand, explode, transform, and disintegrate all at the same time.

What's left is a living Picasso.

One of the crappy ones. But also sprinkled with nightmare fuel. Everyone who bears witness will have nightmares about it, some of them for the rest of their lives.

But at least he's dead.

To his credit, Dorsky rallies the chefs and Boosha through the sanity-testing scene. They break from their skirmish line and terminate the remaining elves and reindeer, with help from Hara.

Ritter occupies himself with Cindy. She has several deep cuts from catching the base of the reindeer's horns, although thankfully none are mortal.

He kneels over her, taking off his coat and bundling it up to compress the bloodiest wounds.

"Did we win?" she asks tightly, obviously fighting to stay conscious.

"I don't think that's an applicable term under the circumstances, Cin."

"I get the assist on that last one though, right?" Moon asks, standing over his shoulder. "I mean, I was *all over* that toss-me-the-bag thing."

"Oh my god shut up so much, Moon!" Cindy yells from where she lies, the force of it prickling her wounds and causing her spine to bend.

Ritter calms her.

She looks up at him earnestly.

"But is it over?" she asks.

Ritter doesn't have an answer.

RED-EYES

"I can't raise anybody," Dorsky says, his tone dark and urgent. "No cells. I call the hotel, they give me the fucking runaround. I can't get a hold of Bronko, Jett, any of them out west."

They're in Bronko's office, Dorsky, Ritter, and Cindy. They entered the sanctum, a firing offense on any normal day, to search for contact information for Allensworth in case of an emergency. No one but Bronko has ever dealt with Allensworth or his people directly. All of their gigs and marching orders came from the chef.

But they can't find anything. There are no numbers, no instructions, no secret red phone.

Nothing.

They've spent the last hour triaging the staff, getting everyone patched up and tucked in safely in Jett's hospitality wing of the building.

Hara and Moon are still on the roof burning all the bodies, even the elves Ryland turned to stone, just to be on the safe side.

The cops seem to know to stay away from Sin du Jour,

but if the police come, they come.

They've got bigger problems right now.

"Are we sure there aren't more of those things coming for us here?" Cindy asks.

She's sitting gingerly on the edge of a plush leather couch big enough for Bronko to crash on when they're in the weeds with a big job. Cindy holds one hand against her side. There are bandages wrapped around her torso from her waist all the way up under her breasts. It's seeping in several places. Ritter wanted her to rest, but Cindy wouldn't relent.

"How do we know anything right now?" Dorsky fires back irritably.

"If there were more," Ritter states with finality, "they would've sent them after us already. That was the point. To wipe us out."

"How do we even know Allensworth hasn't sold us all out?" Dorsky demands.

"We don't! But reaching out is our only option. There's nowhere to hide from this. We need protection."

"It's not an option anyway," Cindy says. "We don't know how to call the man."

"We need Bronko," Ritter says. "We need him to reach out. We need to warn them. We need to make sure they're safe."

"How?" Dorsky asks.

"I'm going out there. Now."

Cindy looks up at him. "Commercial?"

"No. I know a guy with a jet. I can be there by 3:00 a.m. West Coast time."

"Let's go, then," Dorsky says.

"No. You're still in charge here. You've got injured people. You need to stay, fortify this fucking place from top to bottom, and wait. Cindy and Hara'll stay too."

He expects Dorsky to argue, but he just nods gruffly.

Whatever else he is, he's committed to his people, and he respects the chain of command and his responsibilities to it.

"You ain't going alone," Cindy says. "And don't throw me any high-handed bullshit on it, either. I'm not in the mood."

"Fine. If you can make it, let's go."

"Will you get to them in time?" Dorsky asks him, and there's a desperation, a vulnerability in his voice Ritter has never heard before.

"I don't know," he says. "But either way, Hell isn't done getting kicked in the nuts tonight."

He helps Cindy to her feet and the two of them exit Bronko's office, leaving Dorsky there to soak in his role.

"That was a good line," she tells him when they're in the hall. "You were watching *Billy Jack* again, weren't you?"

PART III

THE AFTER-AFTER-
AFTER-PARTY

PROLOGUE, TAKE THREE:
BRONKO IN HELL

Bronko wakes to the sound of his own soul frying in a blazing vat of demon oil, then he smells succulent flesh cooking and realizes it's not his soul; it's bacon. Someone is cooking bacon.

His hands grasp the bare flesh of his own torso and his eyes blink rapidly at the rough surface of a wooden cabin ceiling.

He's back. Bronko instinctually knows it's the truth. He's back in the living, waking world of flesh and blood. His fingers touch the patch of flesh that was expertly pierced by Allensworth's blade. There's a subtle line there, but nothing that feels like the deep stab wound that killed him. It's already a fading memory, and he knows soon there'll be no evidence the wound was ever there.

The first time his soul returned from Hell and he woke up in his body anew, Bronko wept. He curled up in a fetal ball and sobbed until his eyes, nose, and throat were raw and wasted from the letting of tears.

That was many years ago, when the knowledge of his ul-

timate fate was a devastating revelation.

Now, having returned from a brush with eternal torment for a second time, Bronko just feels hollow.

He sits up in bed and looks around the simple guest room in which he's been placed. Bronko stares out through a large picture window behind him. A rolling green countryside stretches to a tree-lined horizon. He must be upstate somewhere.

Bronko finds a plaid robe large enough to fit his stout frame hanging from a simple hook on the door to the bedroom. He leaves the room and follows the cooking smells through what turns out to be much more like a lodge than a cabin, with many rooms and winding halls leading to the top of a staircase. Bronko descends the steps, an open kitchen adjoined to a living room revealing itself as he does.

Allensworth stands in front of a '50s-era gas stove. He's wearing an immaculately pressed Adidas running suit and tennis shoes. He expertly cracks two eggs into a hot frying pan beside another lined uniformly with darkening strips of bacon.

"Welcome back, Byron!" he cheerfully greets Bronko. "Breakfast will be up in a few minutes. I'll thank you not to judge my culinary attempts too harshly. I am, after all, a novice impressionist painting for Renoir here."

Bronko shuffles into the kitchen. "How did I get here?" he asks, each word stinging his dry throat. "And where're we at?"

"Oh, we have our ways. You were spirited off before anyone from your staff saw you . . . incapacitated on your office floor. This is a little getaway I keep for myself. We're a few miles outside of Tuxedo, New York. I wanted you to reenter the mortal plane somewhere comfortable, secluded, and . . . friendly, I suppose."

"How long?" Bronko manages before having to clear his throat. "How long was I . . . gone?"

"Oh, how inconsiderate of me."

Allensworth retrieves a clear carafe and a glass. He quickly places the latter on a round kitchen table draped with a checkered cloth in front of Bronko and fills it with water.

"Please, sit. Drink."

Bronko yanks a chair out from under the table and lurches down into it. He takes up the drinking glass with a trembling hand and gulps the water gratefully, not even caring when he begins hacking up air afterward.

"Three days," Allensworth informs him, returning to the stove. "You missed the rest of the weekend, I'm afraid."

"Me and J.C.," Bronko mutters, pouring himself another glass of water and chugging it down, stifling his gag reflex.

"I also had the large stain in your office attended to. It'll be as good as new upon your return. As to that, you gave your staff an extended weekend off after the trials of Prince Marek and Princess Bianca's wedding this past weekend."

"I did."

Allensworth nods. "Very generously, I must say. They'll all return to work tomorrow, as will you."

Allensworth reduces each burner's flame to nothing and begins loading a plate with the breakfast dishes he's prepared.

Bronko's eyes drift from the man's back to a wooden block beside the stove, from which half a dozen plastic knife handles protrude.

"What would happen if I stabbed you?" he asks Allensworth casually.

Bronko's benefactor shrugs, seeming totally unperturbed by the question or its implication.

"I'd die, I imagine," he says.

"And then what?"

Allensworth sighs, carefully sliding two sunny-side-up eggs onto the plate. "I imagine it's different for everyone, even if the destination is the same."

"I hope not," Bronko says quietly, a deadly edge to his voice. "I hope we end up in the same place someday."

Allensworth remains unshakeable. "Byron, I'm hardly the source of your celestial problems. You created those all on your own, long before we met."

He sets the plate carefully in front of Bronko. "Now, eat heartily. We've got to get you back to work. You've got a new event on the books, something that just cropped up. Something . . . different."

"What is it?" Bronko asks, staring down at the food in front of him with no appetite.

"It's a movie premiere party in Los Angeles," Allensworth informs him brightly. "They've requested Sin du Jour specifically and vehemently. I think you'll find it stimulating. A change of scenary will do you good."

Bronko picks up his fork, but drops it as soon as images of slicing into his own guts seem to scrape the surface of his brain. He has to lean away from the table and blink hard several times to banish them.

"Are you all right?" Allensworth asks him with what certainly sounds like genuine concern.

Bronko nods. "I just hate Hollywood."

"Byron, come now. You adore Hollywood."

"Yeah. Sure. I'll go either way."

As long as I don't have to step foot inside a studio, he thinks.

Bronko's had a belly full of bright lights and television cameras, enough to last an eternity.

BOFFO BOX OFFICE HEAVEN

At the end of the night Producer One summons the chefs, plus Pacific and Mr. Mirabel, to the hotel kitchen where Nikki prepped most of her desserts and dishes for the after-party.

He pops the cork on a bottle of Cristal and pours it into six flutes, handing one to each chef and taking the last glass for himself.

"To the after-after-after-party!" He toasts them.

They all clink their glasses together and drink deeply.

"Damn, that's the stuff," the producer concludes after downing half the contents of his flute.

"It tickles where you want," Bronko agrees.

"You know, I want to share something with you folks. It's . . . not something I'd ever confess to anyone in town, but I feel like y'all are in a unique position to hear me on this."

Lena looks over at Bronko uneasily.

He just shrugs.

"I've been in this business for twenty years. Made . . . fourteen features? Half of them were boffo box office smashes. Grossed something like a combined three billion worldwide."

"What about the other half?"

"Lena!"

Producer drops his aw shucks for a moment, then quickly replaces it with a smile.

"It's cool. It's cool. My point is . . . I've done everything you have to or can do to get your movie made in this town, and I'd say ninety percent of it is shit no one should ever have to do or see."

They all start to laugh, but it quickly becomes apparent he's not exaggerating.

Producer ignores or doesn't recognize the sudden awkwardness.

"And honestly, none of it bothers me anymore. Except for one thing. One thing. Still gets to me. No matter how many times it's necessary for one of my movies I just can't stomach it without about five handfuls of Xanax. And even then I have nightmares."

He stops.

He waits.

He looks at them all expectantly.

Lena is the one who finally asks: "So what is it? What's the one thing?"

The producer takes a deep breath, staring into his glass.

"These goddamn human sacrifice rituals," he says.

None of them attempt even an awkward forced laugh this time. Instead they stare at him in confusion and discomfort, as if he's just told them an overtly racist joke.

"I mean, look," he continues, almost talking to himself now, "I've taken out the occasional assistant or PA or, y'know, try living in Malibu for a decade and not killing a few hookers every now and then, especially when your connect gives you monkey hormones instead of HGH and doesn't fucking tell you till you've already shot your ass full of the stuff. Am I right?"

He laughs then, shaking his head at the memories playing in montage fashion in his own head, an appropriate Kenny Loggins song playing over it.

"But what's going to happen to y'all," he concludes soberly. "It's just . . . it's not right. It's not normal. You know what I mean?"

Lena, of course, doesn't, but by now she's not only confused by his words, she's confused by language itself. In fact, she stopped being able to comprehend words right before the bit about the hookers.

She tries to speak and it's as if she's sucking on the innards of a fresh lemon. She also realizes her hand holding the glass has dropped and spilled the rest of its contents down the leg of her chef's pants.

Lena looks from the stain over at Darren, Bronko,

and the rest, her eyes seeking comprehension more than help.

That's funny, she thinks with that automatic, dream-like acceptance of an absurd reality. She didn't even hear them fall, yet they're all sprawled unconscious on the floor.

It takes much more effort to turn her head this time, to regard the producer, who's grinning at her.

"You know what?" he asks, raising his hand and thrusting a pointing finger at her around the glass. "You're a bad bitch. I can tell. Tough. Not afraid to speak up. I got stuck with a director like you on one of my first movies, before I realized why we don't hire women to direct and had the stroke to make sure it never happened again. She gave me no end of shit about every little bull-shit artistic detail. Used words like 'story' and 'charac-ter agency' and whatnot a lot. Movie tanked, of course. I made sure that cunt never worked again. Hard."

Of course, long before he's done talking Lena has passed out and collapsed on the floor.

The producer looks down at her over his glass. "They'll save you for last. They like breaking bad bitches down. They're a lot like we are. No creativity, though."

He drains his glass, making a satisfied sound as he swallows. The champagne tastes perfect, not a hint of the chemical sedative his assistant added to it that afternoon with a long syringe.

The stuff they used to use gave the champagne a funky aftertaste, and it would make the producer sick for days, despite the medication he took beforehand to neutralize the sedative's immediate effects. He hated that.

He'd have to give his assistant a bonus. Where the kid found this stuff, it was a keeper.

The producer sets his glass down on the prep station top and peers down at the unconscious chefs.

He thunderclaps his hands together.

"All right, kids! It's showtime!"

BELOW THE LINE

Backstage, Producer Two approaches Jett with two flutes of champagne and a dazzling smile.

"Well, I'd call this a grand success," she proclaims.

"Oh, thank you so much! But we haven't even done the finale yet. I've got a thousand silver balloons and the cream for the giant flaming cherries jubilee that's going to drop from the ceiling at midnight!"

"And I cannot wait!" the producer assures her, extending one of the half-filled champagne flutes. "Toast with me."

"Oh, no thank you," Jett says as sorrowfully and sweetly as possible. "I don't drink. The calories, the sugar. My system can't handle it, let alone the booze."

"Oh, come on! One sip, just for me. You've done such a good job."

Jett puts on her most sincere and polite smile. "You know there is like nothing I wouldn't do to please my special clients, but it would just make me sick and those Jimmy Choos you have on are too fabulous and rare to ruin."

The producer sighs, taking back her proffered hand. "That's really disappointing, Jett."

"Oh, I'm so sorry! Really! But thank you. I—"

"Boys!" The producer yells, sounding nothing like the delightful hostess from a moment ago.

Jett looks where the producer is now looking, at one of the black curtains quartering off the area.

Two absolutely humongous men in dark suits and wearing severe expressions step through the curtain. One of them is holding an electric taser in his right hand.

Jett looks back at the producer. "What is this?"

"This is what a line producer does, sweetie," she says blandly.

The man holding the taser advances on her. Jett frowns at the producer before turning away and then abruptly leaping from the spot where she's standing. She bounds at the taser-wielding goon like a gazelle, shouting a bloodcurdling war cry.

The man actually stops advancing, eyes widening in total surprise.

Jett drives the heel of her right palm up under his nose with shocking speed and power, crushing his septum, shattering bones, and causing his head to snap back at a wholly unnatural angle.

The other man is on her immediately, arms widening to encircle her. But before he can begin to close them

Jett has reared back and driven the slim, hard, protruding bone of her forearm into his throat with deep impact. She immediately recharges and unloads several more forearms and elbow strikes on the man's face and skull, but in truth the shock of the oxygen-restricting first blow was enough to send him crumpling to his hands and knees, sucking air that can find no access.

Meanwhile his compatriot, dazed, has dropped the taser and is trying to rub away the tears filling his eyes. His feet shuffle drunkenly. Blood is pouring down his mouth and chin and the front of his suit.

His nose, which naturally pointed slightly down when he walked through the curtain, is now upturned.

Jett whirls furiously on the producer.

"Whoa!" the woman yells, holding up the champagne flutes as if they're shields. "Where the fuck did that come from?"

"I am a single professional woman in New York City!" Jett yells back, sounding more offended than angry. "What exactly about me makes you think I dick around?"

The producer lowers the flutes slightly, staring at Jett in abject wonder.

"Now," Jett demands, "what is this? Are you in some way unhappy with Sin du Jour's service?"

"Wow. Girlfriend, you are fierce, but you aren't very bright, are you?"

Jett frowns again.

She also punches the woman in her mouth.

The producer drops both champagne flutes. They shatter on the floor as she staggers backward, cupping both hands around her bleeding mouth and spitting two teeth between her fingers convulsively.

Jett turns and flees between the disabled bodies of the producer's goons.

THE BREAK OF DAWN

They all wake up suspended high above the ground and with splitting headaches.

Bronko, Lena, Darren, Nikki, Pacific, and Mr. Mirabel are all tied to thick wooden poles cut to equal length and lined up in a perfectly spaced row. Their arms are stretched behind them around each pole and bound at the wrist with tight, heavy bonds. Their feet are perched precariously on tiny ledges nailed to each stake.

"Did he call me a 'cunt'?" Lena asks drunkenly, trying to blink away the haze.

Darren is far away in his own mind, wondering what Lena is cooking for their breakfast. "Who did?"

"Harsh buzz," Pacific complains amiably.

"Moto California es fuerte mierda," Mr. Mirabel agrees, painfully.

Nikki has more pressing concerns. "Hey! Where's my cherries jubilee?"

"All of you, get your heads together," Bronko instructs them. "We're in a fix here."

With his words they begin to examine their current

predicament in earnest.

The giant cherries jubilee Nikki constructed for the grand finale has been removed from the center of the space.

In its place is a five-foot-high platform upon which the stakes they're tethered to have been raised. Several feet below theirs, dry kindling is piled high, covering the platform's surface. In several spots it's bunched around plastic containers marked as chemical accelerants.

Bronko is the first one to realize it's a pyre.

Lena is the first one to say it out loud.

"They're going to burn us alive? Are you fucking kidding me?"

"This is a joke, right?" Darren pleads more than asks. "This is some kind of... Hollywood thing. Or... or YouTube thing?"

"Bronko, what's happening?" Nikki asks, more composed yet no less terrified.

They're all looking to him for the answers, as they often do, as they're supposed to do. He's their chef. He's their leader.

But all Bronko can do right now is shake his head.

He looks from the kindling and accelerant at their feet to the VIP party guests now lining the walls of the space. Some are watching them with a combination of detached interest and mild amusement. Most are ignoring them in favor of chattering among themselves, staring at the screens of their smart phones, and continuing to munch on the appetizers and desserts from the buffet tables.

"They're still eating the food," Bronko can't help marveling. "They're still eating *our* damned food."

He suddenly finds himself laughing, absurdly and maniacally and uncontrollably.

It's somehow more frightening to the other chefs than finding themselves tied to a sacrificial pyre.

The outburst ends as quickly as it began, leaving Bronko hyperventilating slightly, his barrel chest heaving up and down.

"I'm ... I'm sorry, y'all," he says to them, his head hanging in shame and defeat. "I didn't see this coming. Any of it."

"You should have, Chef," a familiar voice half-chastises, half-taunts from far below.

"These other rubes don't know any better," the producer continues, "but you were part of the scene for years, Bronko. You know how it works out here. You should've paid more attention while you were cooking our meals."

He pops a sushi roll into his mouth and smiles as he chews.

Bronko raises his head and closes his eyes, breathing

deeply in and out until he's brought himself back under control.

He opens his eyes and regards the producer coolly.

"They're employees," he says, voice steady and calm. "I'm the boss. I call the shots. I'll stand for them alone."

The producer applauds him. "There he goes thinking like a director instead of a producer, folks. Sorry. It's got to be all of you."

"Says who?" Bronko asks.

The producer sweeps an arm back toward the closed double doors. "More satisfied customers."

Two attendants pull those doors apart and a procession of figures robed in red begins filing inside, dozens of them, all of them carrying medieval-looking torches lit and blazing.

They're the same robes worn by the Oexial clan, the oldest demon collective.

Everyone tied to a stake remembers them immediately, particularly the melée that occurred at a peace accord banquet between them and a younger clan when an Oexial elder choked on food served by Sin du Jour.

The Oexial begin surrounding the raised pyre, chanting low and faint beneath their hoods.

Nikki is the first of them to speak: "Oh, dear."

"We're hosed," Lena agrees.

"Their boss doesn't forgive and he doesn't forget, apparently," the producer informs them.

"Yeah," Bronko says. "I know."

The producer cocks his head to one side, curiously. "You really thought you got away with it, didn't you? Or were you just deluding yourself that you had?"

"What're you getting for this?" Bronko asks, ignoring the question.

The producer shrugs. "Guaranteed billion-dollar worldwide box office. At least five Oscar nods, guaranteed win for myself. Two sequels. *Pirates of the Caribbean*–type shit. The stuff of dreams around the Producers Guild."

Bronko can feel the desperation rising from deep inside him, but he has one last card to play.

"There's no way Allensworth signed off on this. We don't give our own kind to demons or anyone else. That's the oldest rule there is."

The producer. "You really are shockingly naïve. I didn't ask him. Why the hell would I? I'm answering to a slightly higher authority here than a government spook. I'm protected."

"Not from me," Bronko assures him, but the threat is hollow and he most of all knows it.

The producer is even more unimpressed. "Right, yeah. Well, look, they have to do their pre-ritual thing here. Should only take a minute, and then we'll light this candle. Feel free to scream all you want. That's part of it."

The producer turns and slips through the assemblage of demons, returning to the rest of the humans lining the walls.

Lena's head whips toward Bronko. "They're not really going to do this, are they? Not really?"

"Yeah, they really are," Bronko says without looking at her.

"No worries, brah," Pacific says. "I've got this."

He begins shifting the sharp angles of his thin body against its bonds as if trying to reach something behind him.

"What's up, Pac?" Bronko whispers urgently. "Have you got a blade? Can you get free?"

"I almost . . . got it!" Pacific proclaims triumphantly.

Bronko and the rest crane their necks to see.

Pacific tosses something from his restrained hands to the kindling at their feet.

It lands with a soft rustling.

"What was that?" Darren asks.

Mr. Mirabel laughs until it becomes a hacking cough. "His stash," he says.

"Just breathe in when the smoke hits you. It'll make the whole ride easier," Pacific assures them.

"Goddammit, Pac!" Bronko thunders.

"Better than nothin', boss!"

Darren can't grasp the St. Guadalupe medal around his neck with his hands, so he presses his chin into his chest over the precious object given to him by Wela Vargas on the day of his First Communion.

He begins muttering inaudibly to himself, eyes shut tight, lips fluttering with the rapidity of hummingbird wings.

The rasping, unintelligible words draw Lena's attention.

"Darren? Darren! What are you doing?"

"Praying," he answers quickly before returning to the litany.

"Are you fucking serious?"

"Leave him be, Tarr," Bronko instructs.

"No! What are you praying to?" she demands. "What do you think is going to happen?"

Darren opens his eyes and looks up at her, unbelieving.

"How can you ask me that? We . . . we met Him. We touched Him."

Lena is practically vibrating with rage now.

"It was a dog, Darren! It was a fucking stray dog!"

"But the angel—"

"It was a mutant bat! A carnival freak! There're no angels and no God pretending to be a show dog! Grow the fuck up! This is real! This is real and we're all about to die!"

"Lena, that's enough! Please!" Nikki insists, her voice filled with the same compassion that always resonates there, even now.

"Where are all your fucking wonders now, Nikki?" Lena shoots back at her, completely out of control.

"Let it go, Tarr! Now!"

"Uncool, babe," Pacific adds.

Mr. Mirabel begins to agree, but begins coughing and hacking before he can get the words out.

The old man's sudden spasm more than anything seems to snap Lena out of it. She looks around at them all as if seeing them for the first time suddenly.

Then the reality hits her, and she hangs her head silently.

"Fuck!" she curses under her breath.

Around them, the chanting of the Oexial ceases.

One of them breaks from the circular formation of the others. He's the only one not bearing a torch. He draws back his hood, revealing a wrinkled, aging, yet no less imposing demonic visage.

The Oexial elder raises his arms and addresses all of them tied to the stakes.

"For causing the unnatural death of our greatest leader and general, Astaroth, our Lord and Master, the Morningstar of Desolation, has ordained your souls be sent to his terrible grace by fire."

"You suck, dude," Pacific calls down to him.

Several of the other Oexial clansmen hiss under the hoods of their cloaks.

Their elder smiles.

A smiling demon is the opposite of joy.

"Send them home," he softly commands.

All around the chefs and servers staked to the pyre torches touch the kindling. It burns even quicker than they might've anticipated, spreading from the edges of the platform toward the center like a cartoon dynamite fuse.

The heat is immediate and more oppressive than they could've imagined.

"Do like Pac said!" Bronko yells above the rising chorus of demon chants and crackling fire. "Breathe in when the flames get high enough."

Lena can't believe her ears. "Are you fucking serious?"

"If you're lucky," Bronko continues, unabated, "the flames'll collapse your lungs and you'll go out! It's the best we got!"

His intentions and the logic of it cut through Lena's hysteria. She stares directly at him, an unexpected calm seizing her in that moment.

She nods. "Yes, Chef."

Lena looks over at Darren, then at Nikki, glancing

back and forth between them as she says, "I'm sorry. I love you both."

Darren just nods, unable to speak.

"We know how you are," Nikki says, trying even now to sound hopeful, even playful. "We love you, too."

"I'll see you on the other side, Mo!" Pacific shouts at Mr. Mirabel, who just nods, his coughing a ragged constant now.

Lena looks back at Bronko, holding his eyes as deeply as she can. "This isn't your fault. We all made the choice. Don't blame yourself."

Bronko smiles back at her, but it's a twisted smile, warped by sadness and pain. "You don't even know, girl. But thanks."

There are no more words and no more time for them.

The fire hits the accelerant containers, which burst, feeding the flames and causing them to jump five feet all around the stakes, which are now burning.

They feel it on their feet, their ankles, searing their legs and sending shock waves of pain up their bodies.

Darren is the first one to open his mouth to scream, out of fear as much as pain, but his scream is cut off by a much louder, far more surprising sound.

It's the 2013 hit single "Get Lucky" by Daft Punk (featuring Pharrell), all of a sudden blasting from the rafters throughout the entire space.

As it does, expansive netting covering the ceiling reels back and releases thousands of reflective silver balloons, many of which pop as soon as they touch the intense heat and exposed flame of the pyre, but most of which float down between the collected humans and demons now glancing around in confusion.

"I told you to find that hipster party planner bitch!" the producer screams somewhere against the thundering bass of the music. "She—"

The sleekly composed pop song doesn't drown out the rest of his words, they're halted as he stares up and catches a glimpse of the third component to Sin du Jour's epic after-after-after-party finale.

Directly above the blazing sacrificial pyre, aimed at the spot where the giant cherries jubilee dessert stood just an hour ago, a thousand gallons of creamy, gourmet white chocolate pours from the ceiling.

It bathes the chefs first, covering them head to toe before splattering over the entire breadth of the pyre and beyond.

The torrential cream extinguishes every inch of flame with a bubbling chorus of "pops," giving rise to the distinct, but not entirely unpleasant smell of burnt marshmallows.

It even puts out the Oexial clansmen's torches, slathering their ceremonial robes.

After the balloons and cream have settled, the latter still dripping from the edges of the pyre and spreading across the floor, Pharrell's smooth vocals abruptly deepen and elongate and then the song ceases entirely.

No one, not even the demons, speaks.

They don't seem to have the words to describe the last few seconds.

Who would, really?

DIVINE STRIKE

"Goddammit, we're on triple overtime here already, people!" the producer announces irritably. "I've got union grips waiting to mop up a fire we haven't even managed to set yet! Get this shit cleaned away and get new accelerants laid down on the pyre, now! And find Jett Hollinshead! I want her staked up there by the time we're ready to go again!"

"This is the deepest blasphemy!" the Oexial's elder announces from beneath a layer of ceremonial robe covered in a layer of vanilla ganache.

"It's a temporary delay," the producer assures him.

"My warriors will feast on your guts!"

The producer is unmoved. "Yeah? Get in line behind the Teamsters, pal."

"We didn't die, we didn't die, we didn't die," Darren is repeating frantically, gratefully, half his head and face obscured by frothy cherries jubilee topping.

Bronko spits sweet cream from his mouth, blinking it out of his eyes simultaneously. "Jett," he marvels, shaking his head and venting more cream from his hair. "Has to be."

Pacific is chuckling. "This is so gnarly."

"Yeah, great," Lena says, licking away ganache angrily as she speaks. "Only they're just going to wipe this shit away and start again."

Nikki is incensed. "It is *not* shit! That is Malaysian vanilla bean! I cured them myself!"

Lena rolls her eyes. "Christ, Nik, you know what I mean!"

"Oh. Right."

"What're we going to do now, Chef?" Darren asks Bronko.

Humans in coveralls are already appearing from the background with industrial brooms, ready to sweep ganache from the platform.

"I don't know, Vargas," Bronko answers heavily. "Keep praying, I guess."

But it seems Darren has already prayed enough.

The entire room begins to shake, and at first the locals in attendance are ready to brush it off as a minor earthquake.

Then the shaking becomes a steady, wholly unnatural vibrating that reaches all the way to each of their cores.

Then the artisanal skylight high above their heads shatters.

Glass rains from the ceiling torrentially, piercing the

layer of dessert cream covering everything.

A blazing comet streaking down in a perfect, blinding arc follows it.

The ball of fire impacts several yards in front of the sacrificial pyre, cracking the marble floor and creating a wave of cream that splatters the walls in every direction.

The flames flash brilliant and twenty feet high, then extinguish in what sounds like a chorus of harsh whispers.

The world stops vibrating.

What's left is a dissipating jet streak that touches the sky, the faint smell of ozone, and a figure that's stepped straight out of a Biblical painting.

A statuesque woman now stands where the ball of fire made landfall. Her skin is a deep bronze and her hair a mane of dark, glistening curls. She's bolted into resplendent armor from head to toe, every gleaming plate of it embossed with angelic script. In one hand she grips the haft of a halberd, a towering poleaxe crowned with a wicked-looking crescent moon blade. In her other hand she grips the hilt of a broadsword, and as they all look on its long blade bursts into golden flame that crackles on the surface of the steel without actually seeming to touch a single inch of it.

She also has wings.

Giant, majestic, feathery wings that span fifteen feet

across and glow ethereal white.

She couldn't be more an angel if she tried.

The angel looks up at the faces of the Sin du Jour chefs bound to their bottom-blackened stakes and smiles radiantly.

Shockingly, Lena is the first one of them to say, unequivocally and without hesitation, "It's her."

"Who?" Bronko demands.

Lena only shakes her head.

She can't.

"Ramiel," Darren answers for her, in awe.

In response, the divine warrior below them nods her perfect chin just so.

It hits them all then, like a wrecking ball in their cerebrums.

This is the same pitiful, alien creature who was delivered to Sin du Jour, and who the chefs were ordered to butcher and serve to the Oexial and their rival demons.

That creature was an angel stripped of its divinity by the darkest magic and laid bare on the mortal plane under human eyes.

This before them is an angel as humans were intended to glimpse them since the earliest recorded sightings, possessed of that same divinity and wearing it grandly.

Bronko, Lena, Darren, Nikki, Pacific, and Mr. Mirabel

are awestruck.

The rest of the humans in attendance are confused and afraid.

The Oexial, on the other hand, are frothing with rage.

There are shouts and curses and demon lips spitting ancient, inhuman words that must mean "angel" in their dialect.

Rather, pejorative terms for "angel."

Half the Oexial contingent strip away their ceremonial robes. Those that do are also heavily armed and armored beneath, the warrior sect of the clan. They unsheathe curved blades and axes fashioned from what looks like volcanic glass. Their already fearsome teeth have also been filed to even sharper points; many serrated and shaped like small knife blades. They begin encircling Ramiel at a distance, spacing themselves in obviously practiced battle formation.

"Get in there!" the producer yells above the din. "Help them! Take that thing down!"

A dozen humans break from the wall, most of them goons in dark suits like the two "private security" meat slabs that attempted to subdue Jett.

They take up position between the Oexial warriors, armed with tasers, tactical knives, and pistols.

Together they begin closing the net of bodies they've formed, surging in toward Ramiel.

She waits another two seconds, then springs into action.

Her armored feet leave the floor, wings beating so subtly their motion is barely visible, levitating her several feet in the air.

Ramiel suddenly begins spinning like a top on the end of a string, becoming a kinetic blur of motion.

The pole of her halberd extends fully from one hand as she does.

Before they've even realized it, half a dozen of the Oexial warriors and human guards have had their heads separated from their necks.

The force of each strike is such that the bodies hit the floor before their heads do.

~

The other minions manage to leap back past the edge of the sudden killing field.

Several gunshots are fired, the slugs bouncing off her armor harmlessly.

"Converge on the Enochian now!" the Oexial elder commands them. "Drown it in your own blood if necessary!"

The humans hesitate, but the demon warriors surge forth anew.

Ramiel bends at the knees and her wingtips point to the skylight she shattered.

In one frighteningly powerful motion her wings beat down and she launches herself into the air, the sudden and violent updraft knocking several demon and human minions off their feet.

The angel swoops down and cuts a hard turn, flying around the sacrificial pyre and behind the Sin du Jour crew bound to their stakes.

Ramiel extends her halberd and streaks in a perfect horizontal arc, the crescent blade of the poleaxe slicing cleanly through the body of each wooden stake directly beneath the platform supporting each chef's feet.

One by one each length of timber falls forward or to the side.

Everyone except for Mr. Mirabel manages to land or at least brace their fall with their feet.

Ramiel sweeps around the front of the pyre and dives back into the fray, meeting demon and human with halberd and flaming sword.

Pacific is the first to deftly slip his bonds over the top of the fallen stake. He easily brings his tied wrists under his feet to return his arms in front of him.

"Pac!" Bronko yells. "My right boot! Quick now!"

Pacific kneels beside Bronko and dips several fingers into his right boot.

He retrieves a tactical folding knife.

"Whoa, sweet," he says.

"Hurry, boy!"

"Right. Sorry, boss."

Pacific flips the blade out and saws through Bronko's bond.

The chef takes his knife back and quickly returns the favor, freeing Pacific's hands.

Lena, Darren, and Nikki have all worked their bonds and themselves free of the stakes by now. Bronko cuts their ties in succession.

"Boss!" Pacific yells with uncharacteristic urgency. "Mo!"

The young server is on his hands and knees beside Mr. Mirabel, who hasn't moved since his stake tumbled to the pyre's surface.

Bronko runs over to them and drops to his knees, carefully sawing through Mo's restraints.

"I think his arm's broke," Pac says with concern. "Is he breathing?"

Bronko single-handedly rolls the stake away from Mr. Mirabel and they gently lay the elder man on his back.

Lena, without a word, slips between them and kneels at Mo's side, wiping away ganache from his face and mouth. Coupling her hands, she begins to expertly perform chest compressions.

As she does, Bronko looks up, staring past the battle on the floor Ramiel is still winning.

He squints into the human onlookers currently trying to melt into the wall, focusing just in time to see the producers slipping through an anterior door near the towering main doors.

Bronko's attention is pulled back as Mo comes to with a burst of violent coughing.

But at least he's breathing again.

Pacific's usual unflappable demeanor returns immediately. "There ya go, Mo!"

Lena stands, breathing heavily, more from nerves than from the exertion of performing CPR on Mr. Mirabel.

"Tarr, I'm making you responsible for everybody here," Bronko says suddenly. "Lead 'em off this thing and find a back way out of here. I'll meet you at the van."

"What the hell are you talking about? What are you going to do?"

The others begin to protest as well, but Bronko ignores them, focusing intently on Lena.

"You heard me! You're responsible for 'em. All of them. You understand?"

Lena's eyes communicate how absurdly unfair he's being, but there's also no time to argue.

She simply nods.

Bronko stares at her hard and points behind the pyre, at the area of the space where no one is milling or fighting.

Then he takes off in the opposite direction, leaping down from the platform.

"We can't leave without him," Nikki insists, aghast. "We can't!"

"It's his choice," Lena says, turning back to Pacific and Mr. Mirabel.

"Puedes caminar?" she gently asks the old man.

His breathing is incredibly labored, and his arm is in obvious pain, even in the makeshift sling Pacific has fashioned for Mo with his tunic, but he nods.

"Help him," Lena instructs Pacific.

"No worry."

Lena musters the group and prepares to lead them over the back of the pyre, turning to take the lead.

She glances back just in time to watch Nikki's body fold in half, flying back through the air and over the front of the platform as if yanked by an unseen tether.

Lena darts to the edge of the pyre and looks down to see Nikki's prone body obscured on the marble floor by the armored Oexial warrior leaning over her.

Without a conscious thought Lena backs up three quick steps and charges off the edge of the platform, leaping down at the demon warrior and flipping forward in the air. Their backs collide, Lena's momentum enough to knock him forward, off-balance, and send him crashing to the ground.

Lena hits the floor hard and rolls several times before stopping.

When she recovers and looks up she sees Nikki motionless on her side.

The demon she toppled is crouching two yards in front of Lena, snarling furiously at her, curved blade clutched in its hand.

Lena's eyes dart briefly over its shoulder.

Ramiel is very far away, engaged with a dozen more of the things and their human counterparts.

She looks back at the enraged demon warrior covered head to toe in Hell-forged armor, preparing to bull rush her with a killing sword.

There's a quick bubbling of acid in her stomach, and Lena sucks her gut in to squelch it immediately.

The rest of her is steady and calm.

She widens her stance.

Her fists clench and unclench.

"All right," she says resolutely through gritted teeth. "Bring it, then."

PRIVILEGES OF THE DAMNED

Producer One and Producer Two are hotfooting it while still attempting to appear casual down the hall outside the after-after-party.

Oddly, with the doors closed you'd never know there was a holy war between an angelic warrior and a battalion of demons in session.

"Amateurs," Producer One practically spits. "I had them all helpless and unconscious within easy reach of an industrial meat grinder and a whole bunch of ovens. I could've had this whole thing put away an hour ago. But no, they needed the torches and the chanting and all that lily-gilding bullshit."

"Showmanship went out with Technicolor musicals," Producer Two agrees.

"And it should've stayed that way!"

He presses a smart phone to his ear. "Get my car out front in five minutes."

"Four," Producer Two corrects him.

"Fine, four."

He lowers the phone.

"And I'll tell you something else about working with demons—"

A shockingly powerful hand rams each of them between their shoulder blades, sending them both sprawling forward to their hands and knees.

The producers look back over their shoulders.

"Y'all are going to miss the after-after-after-*after-party*," Bronko says.

The producers stand, slowly and cautiously, trading looks and watching him with uncertainty.

They've both just stared directly into the face of the devil himself.

Somehow the darkness in Bronko's face at this moment is far more unsettling.

He moves toward them as they backpedal.

Bronko points a finger at them.

"You hurt my kids," he says in a voice devoid of anything human in the philosophical sense.

"Whoa, buddy," Producer One says. "*You* hurt your kids. You thought you could pull the wool over the eyes of the devil? Who d'you think you are? You're a has-been Bobby Flay. Your arrogance landed you and them here. Not me."

"Let's agree to disagree," Bronko says.

He reaches out and wraps his large hands around the man's throat, totally encompassing it.

"Squeezing" is far too gentle a term for what happens next.

The producer's face is far more surprised than it is pained or in panic or fear.

Strangling always looks so fake in movies, even his.

He simply can't believe the power in Bronko's hands.

His air is cut off immediately. In seconds his eyes are bulging out of his head and the strength below his waist leaves him, his knees sinking to the floor.

Producer Two shrinks back against the wall in horror.

Bronko's eyes never leave the man from whom he's choking the life.

There is no emotion on Bronko's face.

None.

Producer One blacks out, going limp as a rag doll in Bronko's hands.

Bronko maintains every ounce of pressure on the man's neck until he's sure.

Then he casts his body aside.

Bronko exhales, his chest and shoulders heaving from both the effort and all of the emotion he had to repress during the act.

He looks over at Producer Two, his entire face bloodred.

She attempts a smile, but what forms on her face is an expression of abject terror.

"Can I play the girl card here?" she asks meekly.

Bronko nods. "Sure."

It takes one stride to close the gap between them.

The blade of his tactical folder locks in place in one hand.

Bronko sinks it into the same spot on her abdomen where Allensworth stabbed him not that long ago.

She dies the same way Bronko did.

She won't be coming back, however.

He stares down at the bodies of the producers, breathing still as labored as his soul.

Once this would've been an unthinkable act for him to commit. His hands would've faltered. His conscience would've burned with indignation and protest.

Regardless of how evil these people were, Bronko never could've brought himself to harm them, let alone murder them.

That was a long time ago.

The truth is he's damned, he's seen and felt it, and nothing he does can or will change that fact.

And being damned should have its privileges.

THE GUEST OF HONOR

The Oexial warrior charges at Lena at full speed and with a baritone growl, curved blade clenched in one hand.

Lena springs forward to meet him, but quickly ducks low and launches herself into a shoulder roll across the slick marble floor.

She slides across the floor at high speed, aided by the soupy ganache covering it. Her body crashes into the demon's running legs at the knees.

He tries to bend over and swipe at her with the blade, but he finds his legs swept out from under him and his body tumbling over hers before he does.

They end up in a heap upon the floor, Lena trapped under the demon and the Oexial warrior scrambling to recover his balance while keeping her pinned down.

Unable to slip out from under him, Lena's whole purpose becomes grabbing the gauntleted wrist of his sword arm and controlling that short, deadly blade.

As they struggle, Lena looks up briefly above the demon's scarred, grotesque head.

She glimpses the top of the platform just a few feet

away.

She sees Darren poised at its edge, watching her grapple for her life.

His face is contorted, features tight and pained in an expression filled with obvious, frantic desire to help her.

But his body seems totally paralyzed by fear.

He doesn't move.

The Oexial warrior crushes his weight on top of her. Lena rolls back on her shoulders and brings her legs up around the demon's armored body, stretching them so far they rise above his shoulders and she's nearly folded her body in half. Lena wraps her legs around his upper arms, restricting their movement, and hooks her foot under the thing's chin, pressing her shin against the only truly exposed part of the demon's anatomy: its neck.

It may be a creature born of Hell, but it's using a mortal body that requires oxygen to function.

Astaroth, the Oexial elder who choked to death on a chicken bone at the first event Lena helped Sin du Jour cater, taught her that.

The demon's trapped arms wriggle wildly. The blade manages to knick her deeply at the thigh and buttocks in several places, but she ignores the pain.

She reaches up and grasps the warrior's bald, slimy head, digging her nails into its bare flesh and pulling it forward with both hands, increasing the pressure of her shin across the demon's throat.

The thing begins gagging and sputtering, its air supply restricted.

It struggles raucously, but it can't break free or shake Lena loose of her chokehold.

The thing's viscous green blood begins seeping around her fingernails where they only pierce deeper into its pulpy skull.

In one last, desperate attempt, the demon lifts Lena's entire weight several feet off the ground and slams her back painfully against the floor.

Lena groans through clenched teeth, but she only wrenches the choke tighter.

The demon's struggles become weak; eventually they cease as the thing loses consciousness. His body slumps to one side, armor clattering against the marble floor.

Lena rolls with him, maintaining the choke until she's damn sure the thing is out, then she uncouples from it with great effort and rolls away, a yell of something like frustration mixed with rage mixed with victory escaping her lips before she can check it.

Lena lies on her back, panting and bleeding and staring up at the shattered skylight and the utterly calm, starless night beyond it.

Until it's obscured by a thick-bodied figure leaning over her.

It's Bronko.

"You're shit at takin' orders, Tarr," Bronko tells her as he hauls Lena to her feet.

"That's why they threw me out of the army," she says, labored and in all sorts of pain.

She's nearly knocked back off her feet along with the rest of them as the floor suddenly shudders violently beneath them.

The wildly optimistic thought that Ramiel has called for backup crops up in Lena's mind.

It's possible she's never been quite that wrong in her life.

The shuddering of the ground becomes a full-on epileptic convulsion.

It's enough to halt the battle and send the demons and humans left alive falling back to avoid catching a blade to their skulls because they're preoccupied trying to keep their balance.

A web of cracks begins to form in the marble floor in front of the far wall facing the pyre.

Those cracks pull apart until a single seam is ripped across the floor from one end of the space all the way to the other.

With a sound like the yawning of a giant, the seam becomes a world-shaking split that opens up thirty feet wide and descends far past the foundation of the building into the Earth itself.

Half a dozen corkscrews of flame are belched forth from its depths.

They see its horns first, rising above the lip of the sudden tear in the Earth and apparently reality itself, each one the size of a redwood twisted into a bizarre spiral.

The cranium to which they're attached is made of hide as hard as granite and seems to leak bursts of brimstone.

Its face isn't quite a dragon and isn't quite a bull and isn't at all human yet contains something horrifyingly relatable in its eyes and the expression on its mouth.

All of it rests on a body like a bipedal mountain with five-fingered claws that could lance a house.

No introduction is required.

It's the Lord of Darkness himself.

It's the devil.

There isn't a skeptic on Earth who could deny it in that moment.

Imagine knowing—not fearing, not believing, not feeling, but *knowing* without a single doubt or the slightest ability to deny—that any and every form of joy is a lie. Happiness doesn't exist. Love isn't an illusion, it's a cruel absurdity. Warmth is something that died long ego, an abstract, obsolete truth like dinosaurs or the big bang. You can't remember what it felt like, and, worse, you—don't expect to.

Reality is a barren waste. The only sensation is cold. The only feeling is misery. The only hope is unfulfilled longing that stretches beyond the end of human experience.

All of this is what suddenly composes the world of every human in the room, and it crumples them inward like dead stars. A very real physical weight grips their hearts and presses down on their minds. They're each floored as if gravity in the room has just increased a thousandfold.

The Oexial soldiers and elders sink to the floor as well, but they do so in supplication, immediate and without hesitation.

Ramiel is the only one left standing. She strides forward defiantly, demon blood staining her celestial armor and the ethereal feathers of her wings. It drips from the blade of the halberd, burns black and charred on the blade of her flaming sword.

Standing a dozen feet from the abyss, she stares up at the construct's face unabated and raps the other end of her poleaxe against the cracked marble floor challengingly.

The devil laughs, the sound a thousand rusted chariots driving hard off a cliff into a crackling inferno.

"You look ridiculous," Ramiel says, speaking for the

first time, and with a voice that sounds like a powerful wind moving through caves. "You still love putting on the horns and flame show, don't you?"

The idling devil moves then, with inhuman speed and deeply terrifying purpose. One clawed hand as wide as Ramiel is tall swipes her off her feet. She tumbles awkwardly through the air, wings folded unnaturally around her, and collides with the far wall sickeningly before falling to the floor with a clatter like the sound of a car crash.

Her holy weapons are banished from her hands to opposite sides of the room.

Her flaming sword is extinguished.

She doesn't get up.

From her own place on the floor Lena manages to angle her head just enough to spot Ramiel's unmoving form.

Whatever is more permanent and formless than death, Lena wishes for it in that moment.

The Oexials kneeling before their master begin chanting in a language that scrapes human ears like the edge of a blade. Their bodies genuflect in time, the rhythm and their bloodred robes giving them the appearance of a single undulating organism.

"We ask no mercy for this sacrilege, Master," their eldest elder announces with grandeur. "But your offerings have not slipped the hook. Take them, and us, as you see fit."

The doors don't fly open, they shatter completely, raining shrapnel on human and demon alike.

For a moment it's as if air has been let back into a total vacuum.

The devil actually recoils, just a hair, but it's enough to release the vicelike grips on all of their hearts.

Silence settles over the space.

Then, in the distance, a gentle skittering.

It sounds like tiny feet falling on marble.

Several tiny feet.

In the next moment all the demons gasp and writhe as, through the tall, empty arch where the doors used to be, a small, slightly unkempt Shih Tzu putters into the room.

CANIS EX MACHINA

Its presence causes the demons to moan in severe pain even as it allows every human to breathe easier and feel the barest inkling of hope again.

The devil watches the tiny dog with an undeniable pause that might even be fear.

The Shih Tzu putters up to within a few feet of the chasm in the floor and settles gently on its hind legs.

It stares up at the uncontested master of evil passively, its head slightly cocked.

The chefs find they can move again. Lena begins to lift herself sluggishly from the floor.

Several feet away, Darren struggles with the same action, his eyes on the dog.

"Is that . . . ?"

Lena just nods with as much defeat as relief in her body.

"Dip me in shit and roll me in sugar," she hears Bronko moan with genuine wonder.

It's the same "stray" dog the Sin du Jour staff took in just before Lena and Darren came in that first day for their interview.

It's the same dog that caused an Oexial elder to choke on a chicken bone before he could expose the fact that Sin du Jour had replaced the angel flesh they were ordered to serve at a demon banquet with a Chicken Nuggies substitute.

It's the same dog that freed Ramiel from a magical prison more ancient and powerful than any of Sin du Jour's wizards and alchemists could quantify or understand.

It's also God, whoever or whatever such an entity really is.

It's the God Puppy.

There is no denying it.

The devil speaks in a voice designed to suck the soul from the listener, but somehow it's not as awful as it should be, almost as if its power is being drained as soon as each word leaves him. The words themselves almost sound like questions, albeit in nothing any human would recognize as language.

He's addressing the God Puppy directly.

Again, silence.

The Shih Tzu barks, gently, just once, up at the Lord of Evil.

Whatever answer has been given sends the devil into a sudden terrifying rage. Its hide crackles and burns. Its eyes are lightning. It flails its limbs and unleashes a stream of thundering, inhuman curses.

It's like watching a calm day become a category-10 tornado right in front of you.

All the humans who were finding their feet drop back to the floor, curling up and shielding themselves from it.

The God Puppy merely licks its own face and waits.

Now the devil dips its horrible form over the edge of the chasm, until its face looks as if it will engulf the small animal.

Its huge, bonfire eyes flash and its voice becomes the sound of the world's end as it screams over the dog's insignificant form.

The God Puppy sniffs adorably, waiting.

Whether the devil's tirade runs out of words or steam is any human's guess, but it finally ceases.

The Desolate One stares silently and menacingly at his only true foe.

A low rumble begins in the God Puppy's chest. It builds until his fuzzy muzzle trembles with a gentle growl.

The growl builds until the God Puppy lifts its head high and lets loose an absurdly high-pitched, single bark.

It's as if the devil's form has been hit by an antiaircraft missile.

The rest of them feel it too. The demons scatter. Some

flee the room, others simply fling themselves into the fiery chasm.

For the humans it's more powerful than the devil's presence and in exactly the opposite way. It's like being shown the most powerful truth in the universe, and it cuts straight through the false darkness with which the devil's nearness imbued them.

Hell's commander in chief sinks back into the crater that heralded his entrance into our world, disappearing into volcanic bursts of fire that are extinguished in his wake, leaving the chasm a cold, dark depression leading to nowhere.

Bronko is the first one to make it all the way back to his feet. He stares at the rip in the earth, trying not to look at the God Puppy directly as he absently brushes cream slather and blood from himself.

"Nikki!" Lena's uncustomary terrified shriek cuts through the silence violently.

Bronko whips around to see her cradling Nikki's motionless, rag doll–like form. Blood has soaked through the entire lower half of her smock and the top of her pants. There's a deep puncture wound in her abdomen.

"Nikki?" Lena practically begs, checking her vitals with military precision despite her rapidly deteriorating composure. "Nikki? Nikki! No no no no no no no not you not you not you NIKKI!"

Her screeching descends to unintelligible, manic sobbing. She clutches Nikki's lifeless body close and buries her face in the dead woman's neck, her crying muffled there as her body rocks and shudders.

Bronko manages the few broad strides between himself and their coupled forms.

Then he drops to his knees.

With a haunted, vacant expression he watches Darren crawl to within a foot of the two women as well, registers that the overwhelming emotions dominating the boy are shame and guilt.

A hand on Bronko's shoulder, the sensation of physical contact feeling very distant and removed.

It's Jett.

It's the first time Bronko has ever seen his sous-chef weep.

Pacific, supporting Mo with most of his weight, limps them both close to the others.

Mo crosses himself, tears both of physical pain and grief staining his wrinkled, age-spotted cheeks.

Pacific isn't crying, but his is the most deeply troubled expression Bronko has ever witnessed the young server wear.

Lena abruptly pulls her tear- and blood-slicked face from Nikki's neck and screams at the top of her lungs, a violent, guttural sound filled with as much rage as sadness or loss.

It's a rage born of helplessness.

None of them say a word as her exhausted scream dissipates.

Then, in its silent wake, that gentle skittering of padded feet on the marble.

The God Puppy putters between Bronko and Jett, then bounds up to the other side of Nikki's body.

He rears back on his hind legs and places his front paws gently on Nikki's thigh.

The dog's intelligent, slightly sad eyes peer up at Lena.

She stares down at him through a waterfall distortion of tears, her body still shaking, arms involuntarily constricting around Nikki.

"What?" she manages raggedly. "What do you want? She's dead! She's dead and you're a fucking dog and what good is that? What good are you?"

"He saved us, El," Darren says softly, desperately.

"From what?" Lena demands, looking from the dog to Darren to the rest of them, so much hate etched on her face. "Didn't he make all of this? Didn't he? Then what good is any of it? What the fuck is the point?"

None of them can answer that.

The dog barks, and Lena's attention snaps back to him.

"What?" Lena bitterly demands. "Just fucking talk to us!"

"Lay her down, child," a new voice, melodious and out-of-time, bids Lena.

It's Ramiel.

She's standing in front of the other chefs, seeming unharmed for the blow she sustained.

In fact, the blood is gone from her wings and armor.

Lena looks up at her, taken aback, even in her consumed state.

"Lay her down," the angel repeats, her tone that of a loving parent speaking to a wounded child. "All will be as it should."

"We saved you," Lena says, and it sounds like an accusation.

Ramiel nods. "And so you did. Now do as I say. Please. Lay her down and leave her rest."

More than seeing it, Lena can feel the wisdom, compassion, and divinity contained in the winged creature.

And she doesn't give a shit.

"Fuck you," she says miserably, turning her attention back to Nikki's body. "Fuck all of you."

In the end it's not the forces of Hell that move her.

It's Bronko.

His impossibly powerful hands seize her shoulders, prying her away from Nikki.

As he does, Jett is there behind her, guiding Nikki's head and shoulders gently to the floor.

Lena shrieks and curses and protests, but Bronko's grip is iron. He forces her to her feet and backs her away from where Nikki lies.

"Let it go, girl," Bronko instructs Lena through teeth gritted from the effort of controlling her. "Give 'em a chance."

As they all look on, the God Puppy crawls his front paws up Nikki's body to her shoulder. He sniffs at her ear. His tiny button nose briefly nudges hers.

Finally, he licks her cheek.

Nikki inhales deeply, her eyes opening wide as life returns to her body in an instant.

Lena stops struggling against Bronko's grip, and whether because of that fact or out of his own surprise he releases his hold on her.

Everyone, Lena included, stares in struck silence as Nikki sits up on the stained, shard-covered floor.

She doesn't cough or sputter or convulse.

There is no pain.

She seems refreshed.

The God Puppy turns his head up at Lena and barks.

Her eyes are pulled away from Nikki, and she looks from the dog to Ramiel, questioningly.

"The Giver's words are not your words," the angel explains. "They can never be. Not truly. However, the nearest your words might capture their feeling would be . . . 'you only get one.' Understand?"

Lena nods, dumbly, yet somehow she does.

The God Puppy sniffs, as if in assent.

With that the Shih Tzu hops over Nikki's prone legs and trots across the space to where the buffet table still stands. It leaps up onto the tabletop beside a half-depleted display of cupcakes and begins licking frosting from the top of one.

Ramiel soon joins the God Puppy, picking up a cupcake and gingerly peeling away its wrapper with the same fingers that were swinging sword and axe not ten minutes ago. She bites into the silken confection with unabashed pleasure.

"Come on, girl," Bronko says, scooping Nikki up in his arms easily and cradling her like a child.

"I can walk, Chef," she assures him, confused. "What—"

She finally looks around, taking it all in.

"What happened? Are we . . . what's going on?"

"We're leaving, is what's going on," Bronko says with finality. "Everyone. Let's go. Now. Talk later."

They all obey without question, even Lena. The procession makes its way across the carnage scrawled on the floor in the fouled dessert topping Nikki spent so much time and care preparing.

No one stops them.

No one is left to stop them.

Darren is the last one through the shattered doorway.

His final glimpse of the scene is Ramiel, half-eaten cupcake in one hand, using the other hand to scratch behind the dog's ear.

EPILOGUE:
"A" FOR EFFORT

Lena sits at the foot of the bed in her plush, modern, black-and-white suite with its inexplicably Oriental-influenced design touches.

She's staring blankly at the wall.

She has been for almost an hour straight.

The last truly conscious action Lena took was to hug Nikki down in the lobby before they parted ways. Lena clung to her for the briefest moment, willing tears not to return to her eyes. Nikki giggled in her ear and told her it was okay, that everything was okay now. Allensworth's people had arrived and filled the hotel. They were safe. Bronko even said so.

Lena didn't say anything, but she finally let go and took the elevator up to her room.

She managed to shower. She managed to scrub away the blood, both human and demon, along with the bits of glass and dried dessert cream. She managed to wash her hair for the first time in four days. She managed to dry herself thoroughly and wrap herself in a complimentary cloudlike robe embossed with the Roosevelt Hotel logo. She managed to walk from the bathroom to the foot of the four-post bed and ease herself onto it without her knees buckling.

Then everything seemed to seize, and her brain and body collectively agreed they were done.

Far away in her mind a scene keeps replaying, an old memory lingering like the echo in a canyon.

In Iraq, the drivers of military convoys were instructed not to stop under any circumstance unless ordered, even and especially if a child ran out into the middle of the road.

Lena's unit was riding shotgun for a Halliburton convoy the day a driver ignored that order when a five-year-old holding a rubber ball darted in front of their truck. The driver stopped dead rather than run the boy over.

Five seconds later an IED ripped apart the front of the vehicle with concussive force that became engulfing flame.

Lena survived. She survived that and a lot more before she came home, and at the end of the day the fire and blood and death weren't what disturbed her the most about that convoy attack.

It was the knowledge the driver had been wrong not to run over a small child.

It was not being able to deny that fact.

It was having to live in a world where that was true, whether Lena wanted it to be or not.

That's how she feels now.

So many huge, horrible things are true whether she wants them to be or not.

She can't deny them anymore.

That's the worst part, far worse than almost being incinerated alive along with the only people in the world she really cares about.

A knock at the door, tentative and hesitant.

She knows that it's Darren.

Lena forces herself to stand and cross the room, opening the door and finding him there, also cleaned up, changed into jeans and his favorite T-shirt.

He enters wordlessly, walking past her to the middle of the room and looking around as if he's actually interested in her scattered belongings or the décor.

Lena closes the door and joins him.

His eyes finally work up the nerve to find hers.

They stare at each other silently.

"Are you okay?" he asks.

"No," Lena says, flatly and honestly.

Then they're laughing. It's brief and haunted and without volume, but it's earnest.

It ends when Darren begins to cry.

"I'm sorry," he says hoarsely, holding a hand over his eyes. "I should've done . . . I should've helped you. Helped Nikki. I was afraid."

Lena embraces him before he's done speaking, holding him tightly.

"I was wrong about everything," she tells him. "Everything I said to you. I was wrong and you were right and I'm sorry."

They hold each other, drawing what comfort and catharsis they can from their shared years and history and the closeness of each other's presence.

It lasts as long as it needs to, and then Darren says they should both get some sleep.

Lena agrees, and escorts him to the door.

"Where do we go from here?" he asks her, hand on the doorknob.

Lena shakes her head. "I have no fucking idea, man. We're alive, so we'll go forward. We'll figure out the rest back home."

Darren nods, seemingly genuinely comforted by that. Her confidence has long been his main source of same.

Darren lets himself out, shutting the door and testing the lock from the outside.

Lena walks over to the window, looking down on the lights of Hollywood Boulevard, the tides of tourists trampling the vaunted memorial stars up and down the sidewalks that are a million times dirtier than they ever look in movies or on television.

She sees an abundance of people pushing baby strollers.

Who the hell keeps a baby up past midnight, even on vacation?

Knocking at the door again, this time forceful and deliberate.

"Did you forget something?" Lena asks as she crosses the room and opens it, expecting to find Darren standing there.

It's Ritter.

"I guess I'm a little late, huh?" he says in his typical deadpan way.

"A little bit, yeah," Lena confirms.

She involuntarily pulls her robe tighter together over the top of her chest, realizes she's doing it, and stops.

"This is obviously a bad time—"

"Come in," Lena says automatically, stepping aside.

Ritter enters the room and she closes the door after him.

He turns to her and slides his hands deftly into the front pockets of the weathered black BDU pants he's wearing.

"Is the whole team here?" Lena asks.

"Yeah. Checking in. I talked to Bronko. We'll all stay

the night and head home tomorrow."

"Is everyone back at the kitchen okay?"

Ritter nods. "That's a whole other story, but yeah. Dorsky's fine," he adds.

Lena frowns. "I didn't ask about him."

"That's right. You didn't."

Lena begins smoothing back her hair, again realizes what she's doing, and stops.

"Goddammit," she curses under her breath.

"What?" Ritter asks, brow furrowed just so.

"Nothing."

"You look fine."

"I don't care," she snaps automatically.

"Okay."

They stare at each other in the awkward silence for a bit, until Ritter finally says, "I'll let you be, then. I just wanted to . . . I don't know . . ."

He actually grins, just a little, and there's something just so damn adorably rueful in it.

"It seems like I keep trying to save you, and you keep saving yourself before I get the chance."

"Then stop trying," Lena says flatly.

Ritter nods. "Yeah. I should do that. Lesson learned. Anyway. I'm glad you're whole. I'm glad everyone's whole."

"Then why did you save me?" Lena asks. "I wasn't the

only one trapped inside the office with horny monsters or tied to a stake on a bonfire. You came to save everybody, not just me."

"That's true. I suppose you're the one comes to mind first lately."

Lena is genuinely curious when she asks, "Why?"

Ritter sighs. "I suppose this is the part where I say you remind me of somebody, but that's not true. I guess you remind me of somebody I wanted to meet. Somebody who looks like they've seen a lot of the same shit I have, and had the strength to make different choices on their own when they could've otherwise turned as ugly as the world around them. And who's a helluva lot prettier than me."

Despite herself, Lena likes that answer.

She likes that answer a lot.

All of it.

"I didn't mean that before," she says, probably less guarded than any time she's spoken to him in the past. "I mean, I *don't* need you to come save me. But I appreciate the effort. I see how loyal you are to your people. I respect that."

Ritter smiles.

It's the first real smile she's seen grace his features.

"Thanks for saying. I'll see you downstairs for breakfast with the others in the morning before we all take off, all right?"

Lena nods.

She nods several seconds longer than she normally would.

When she finally stops she says, "Oh, fuck it."

She reaches up and tangles her fingers in his hair with one hand, pulling his face down to hers and kissing his mouth full on.

Genuine surprise slows Ritter's reaction.

He gets over it quickly.

A few moments later Lena sheds the robe she so demurely cinched when she opened the door.

In the morning they'll order breakfast up for just the two of them.

About the Author

Photograph by Earl Newton

MATT WALLACE is the author of *The Next Fix, The Failed Cities,* and his other novella series, *Slingers.* He's also penned over one hundred short stories, a few of which have won awards and been nominated for others, in addition to writing for film and television. In his youth he traveled the world as a professional wrestler and unarmed combat and self-defense instructor before retiring to write full-time.

He now resides in Los Angeles with the love of his life and inspiration for Sin du Jour's resident pastry chef.

TOR·COM

Science fiction. Fantasy. The universe.
And related subjects.

*

More than just a publisher's website, *Tor.com*

is a venue for **original fiction, comics,** and

discussion of the entire field of SF and fantasy,

in all media and from all sources. Visit our site

today—and join the conversation yourself.